EXTRACTION

Rita Britton

PublishAmerica
Baltimore

© 2009 by Rita Britton.
All rights reserved. No part of this book may be reproduced, stored in a retrieval system or transmitted in any form or by any means without the prior written permission of the publishers, except by a reviewer who may quote brief passages in a review to be printed in a newspaper, magazine or journal.

First printing

All characters in this book are fictitious, and any resemblance to real persons, living or dead, is coincidental.

PublishAmerica has allowed this work to remain exactly as the author intended, verbatim, without editorial input.

ISBN: 978-1-61582-602-5
PUBLISHED BY PUBLISHAMERICA, LLLP
www.publishamerica.com
Baltimore

Printed in the United States of America

CHAPTER ONE

Every day was getting to be the same. Mabel would get up and go to the coffee pot and wait for it to finish brewing. She would have two cups and then go shower. After her shower, she would drink the last cup while browsing the newspaper. She looked hard into the classified ads to see if anything struck her as being right for her. Day after day, she sent out resumes and cover letters to try to get a job. Most of the time no one responded. In eleven months she had five interviews and all of them were for low paying jobs and she found herself "overqualified."

She was beyond desperate. She was becoming depressed. Her best friend was diagnosed with breast cancer and was having a difficult time keeping track of her husband. She was sure that he was seeing someone else and did not want to open the Pandora's box while she was suffering from the cancer. So, she filled in Mabel as to his exploits. She told her that she had seen some of his e-mails and that he was soliciting a female for sex. Mabel never liked him but had to keep her mouth shut for fear of alienating her friend. She knew that this kind of mess often resolved itself and her opinions were neither required nor needed. As a friend, she listened while trying to decide how she would make next month's house payment and/or car payment.

The job she had for years in the hospital was gone. They had "downsized." Whatever that was. It meant no more job, no more income, and no more future. Two days before Christmas. Merry Christmas. Bah! Humbug! 2

The savings were at an end and there was no inkling of a job in the near future. She searched the "careers" section and the Chicago jobs section of the internet to no avail. She sent a cover letter to a junior college to try to fill an English teacher position. She made the cover letter humorous in an attempt to catch the eye of whoever read this. She waited and waited.

Dark thoughts invaded her mind. Suicide. Bank robbery. Liquor store holdup. She visualized the foreclosure of her house. Her beautiful little house that she had worked so hard to make comfortable and cozy. Her grass was always cut and her flowers were a show unto themselves. She had put in a pond and the fish were thriving. She spent many summer evenings with a lit fire near the pond listening to the water fall from the filter. She loved living alone with her books and computer. Two divorces made her cynical and often had to bite her tongue in martial subjects her friends wanted to discuss. She knew of no happy marriages and it seemed that couples only tolerated each other often for the sake of their children. If there were no children, they seemed to tolerate each other for the sake of finances. Marriage was not her "thing."

Alone, she could travel whenever the mood struck her and eat when she felt like it. Sometimes she made a sandwich instead of cooking an entire meal. On some days she spent hours trying a recipe for gourmet meals. She like her life. She and her friend, Sue, spent countless hours at flea markets or garage sales looking for a rate tidbit. Sometimes they found a real gem and other times they found nothing but it was their day to waste with no one to answer to.

Sometimes, Mabel thought of her only son who lived out of state with his wife and three children and how she had sacrificed to raise him and send him to college. She ate the same stew for a week in order to save pennies. She wore the same sweatshirt jacket for four years because she could not afford a winter coat. Well, he certainly made it now. He was a pilot for a large airline and was making in the six figure range. He owned a ranch and a few horses. His kids were in every activity imaginable and his wife knew how to spend what he earned.

When her son found out that Mabel had lost her job two years before retirement, he sent her a check for a hundred dollars. Mabel laughed aloud when she opened the envelope and thought that this was truly absurd to say the least. A hundred did not pay for much more than paper towels, toilet paper and Kleenex.

After Mabel finished shopping, she again contemplated the suicide "out" as she thought of it. I could hold a gun to my chest and pull the trigger and know that my heart would have a big hole in it. She had read too many times people shot themselves in the head and ended up paraplegics or with permanent brain injuries. She could swallow pills but she really did not have anything lethal in her medicine cabinet. Cutting her wrists was out completely because she abhorred the mess this

EXTRACTION

would leave for someone to clean. Hanging was sloppy and she had no rafters or beams to tie a rope. She could drive her car into a bridge but with her luck she would total the car and walk away unscathed. No, she needed something that would work and look like an accident. She did not want Sonny, her son, to feel bad about her afterwards. She had exactly one month left to make a decision and then all the money would be gone and she was not going to become homeless and live on a park bench.

Mabel had her first job at the age of 15 and had never been unemployed since. Often she had two jobs and liked it. She had put herself through school while working full time as a sheriff deputy. After her divorce, she needed a man's job and a man's salary to support the kids. Her ex did not pay a dime of court-ordered child support. She was the first female to work with all male inmates. While working at the jail, she got her Bachelors degree. She was forty-five when she got her Masters degree in counseling and kept working and going to school. She did therapy with Domestic Violence offenders until her partner started using cocaine and everything fell apart. But it was only part-time work so she still had a full time job to fall back on. When her second husband and she opened a counseling agency she did not know that he was seeing another woman and every penny she earned he spent in his "bimbo." After six months of being open and running, they lost the building and all the clients. She packed her belongings and moved into her own apartment. Hubby lost the house and wanted to come back to Mabel. She turned him down and wished him luck as she filed for her final divorce.

At first, being on her own was difficult No one needed her. She adjusted quickly and decided that movies and books were great company. Her girlfriends and her formed a card club and on Friday nights played penny poker. She listened to their complaints about the "slobs" they were married to and felt very smug in her own status.

She shopped around for a little house and found it on the first try. The house wasn't on the market yet when the realtor showed it to her. It was blue with white trim and had a lit up lantern on the front lawn with her address on it. It was love at first sight. Sonny came for a visit and approved her purchase and congratulated her with obvious relief because she did not want to move in with him. He came to stay with her for a week so that he could study for the pilot's exam because his house was noisy and distracting with the kids around. At first Mabel was pleased to have him to herself but soon realized that this was no longer the fun-loving boy she had raised. This was a demanding, selfish and cheap human being and were he not her son, she probably would not even like him. He did not want to take her dinner because it was too expensive. He wanted the television off because he was studying. He wanted what he wanted whenever he wanted it. At the end of the week, she kissed him goodbye and was glad to get her house back to herself.

The following summer she went to visit Sonny and told him that she wanted to stay in a motel but he insisted that she stay in his camper by the lake. She was reminded repeatedly that it cost $17.00 a day to camp there. Mabel had driven there with Sue and they pretty much ignored his complaints. They swam and fished and at night would sit by the lake sipping wine and making S'mores over the open flames in the fire pit. They shopped during the day and the grandkids got brown while visiting. Then one night Sonny invited them for dinner and while they dressed they laughed over the fact that he was actually going to spend money on them. They went to an unusual restaurant that served only one meal but was all you could eat. The never ending fried chicken kept reappearing whenever the dish was empty and the mashed potatoes were plentiful. Corn on the cob, dripping with butter and homemade rolls were loaded on plates. They ate until they were ready to pop. The bill came and Sonny said, "Geeze Ma, I forgot my wallet at home." Sue started laughing and said that she had left her purse in the camper.

Mabel picked up the tab and paid sixty seven dollars for a home cooked meal for all. Another lesson learned.

Sue and Mabel had been friends for thirty some years and were closer than sisters. They knew each others' secrets and kept them. Sue knew that Mabel was contemplating suicide and kept putting hope into her that a job would soon be forthcoming. She told her that she would be really upset if Mabel did something stupid like kill herself. She pointed out that she had lost her job and was doing sales on E-Bay to supplement her income from the government. She told Mabel that her friend Marie, the lady with breast cancer, would probably give up if she did not have Mabel's support. Sue tried to come up with any and all arguments against suicide but Sue did not tell anyone. Sonny stopped calling because he could not handle the fact that his mother might need to depend in his support. Mabel knew that they would drive up for Christmas in order to collect the gifts from all the relatives.

Christmas had always been a Large holiday in their house. Traditional cookies and meals were always in the oven. Decorations laced both the outside and inside if the little blue house. Great piles of gifts were always under the tree and this year there would be nothing. No meals, no cookies, no gifts, no grandma Mabel.

She missed all of Christmas due to the flu. She vomited and excreted everything in her system for days. Her son thought that coming by would be great if he did not have to come into her house. This way he could get the gifts and not put his family at risk of getting the flu. Mabel allowed him to get the few items she had bought and he gave her an envelope with fifty dollars in it. "My own little hell, "she thought and continued to vomit until tears ran down her face. She gave herself until the fourth of January to either die or get a job.

CHAPTER TWO

Mabel had purchased a few items from the grocery store to tide her over the New Year's holiday. She kicked her door shut and realized that the door did not shut properly. She fiddled with the lock and finally got it set. She turned around and a huge black man stood in her kitchen holding a very shiny gun at her. She gasped in surprise and smiled. "Maybe I don't have to do the suicide thing if I can get him to do it." She proceeded to put groceries away. He growled at her and said, "What the hell is the matter with you?" He looked vicious and intimidating. He was about six feet and around two hundred solid pounds. He seemed to have no fat on him. His hair was short and neatly trimmed. Mabel smiled at him and started peeling potatoes.

"What are you doing?" he growled.

She smiled at him and said, "I'm peeling potatoes and then I will peel carrots and cut up an onion and celery."

EXTRACTION

"Lady, I'm here to rob you and you peel potatoes. I could kill you." He seemed surprised at his own confession.

She shrugged and stated, "You go ahead and take what you want. I have a VCR, a T.V. and some old movies. There is no cash. No wait," she went to her purse and stated matter-of-factly, "I lied. I do have cash. It's exactly twelve dollars and forty two cents."

She held it out to him. He slapped her hand away.

"You're more pitiful than me, "he said.

"Oh, well. I guess that leaves you having to kill me. Right?" she asked.

He looked at her, totally confused. He frowned up and asked, "Do you want t die?"

She shrugged. "I don't get this." He said puzzled.

He went on, "Most people would be crying and begging for me not to hurt them and what do you do? You peel potatoes." He started a rumble in his chest that exploded into the loudest laugh she had ever heard. He had tears streaming down his face and could not seem to stop the laughter.

Mabel looked at him in astonishment and soon found his laughter infectious and started giggling also. The two were like two people who should have been committed. He put the gun into a holster at his side and proceeded to wipe his face with a sparkling clean cotton handkerchief. When he caught his breath, he asked, "What is your story? I don't scare you and you seem to think that peeling potatoes will stop me from doing what I came to do." He seemed completely confused.

Mabel smiled and replied, "Dying isn't scary when you face destitution."

"What are you talking about?" He queried.

She explained what had been happening and her lack of hope in a future and as she spoke, he nodded as though he understood. She went to the fridge and pulled out salami and cheese and some mayonnaise and a head of lettuce. She placed these in front of him and added two colas. She started making two sandwiches and handed him one while talking the whole time. She explained about her son and his cheapness. He nodded and chewed. She finally finished and bit into her own sandwich but the tears started coming and she had trouble chewing and sniffling at the same time. He pulled out another handkerchief and handed it to her. She thanked him and unceremoniously blew her nose into it. She started laughing and this time he didn't understand. He asked, "What's so funny?"

She answered, "I just blew my nose into my killer's hanky and thanked him." They both started again. He, with his rumbling chest deep roar and she, with her giggling. She brought out stew meat and threw it into a frying pan and added some margarine to brown it. "What's your name?" she asked him.

"Clarence." He rumbled.

She started another fit of laughing and said, "No wonder you're a killer with a name like that. What was the matter with your mother giving you such a sissy name?"

He smiled and said, "That name taught me how to fight from first grade on."

"I believe it"

"What's yours?"

"Mabel."

"That ain't real hot either." He laughed. "Mabel, Mabel strong an able, get you elbows off the table."

"I haven't heard that in years." She said smiling.

"What are you cooking?"

"I'm going to make stew."

"I love stew. My grandma used to make the best. She would add rye bread to it. Do you?"

"Yes. You're welcome to stay for some if you feel up to it."

"I have nowhere to go."

"Why do you do the gun thing?" She asked.

"I have no other choice, "he said. "It's a long story."

"Stew takes hours. I'm listening." She encouraged him.

Clarence started out by telling her that he was the first in his family to finish High School and his Mom was proud of him the day he walked to get his diploma. She cried with joy. The joy was short-lived. His High School sweetheart announced that she was pregnant with his child. He married her at eighteen and became a father six months later. The baby was a girl and they named her Gloria. She was the apple of his eye. He got a job in a grocery store and a part-time job in a local drug store. He had applied for a postman job and was waiting to take the test. One year after he applied, they called. He passed the test and walked for long hours in the blazing heat and freezing rain to support his family. Gloria was thriving and was walking and babbling. He loved her with all his heart. He wiped his eyes as he told her of coming in the door and Gloria clinging to his leg trying to reach him for a kiss. He would swing her in the air and she would squeal with laughter. The High School sweetheart soon got tired of married life and shattered his life by telling him that Gloria was not his but rather another guy she had been seeing at the same time. When she found herself pregnant, the other guy disappeared. But, he was back in town and wanted to see his child. Clarence was shattered. The little girl he loved was not his. At work, an investigation was going in regards to postmen dumping junk mail and he got caught up in it. He came home one day and found no furniture, no toilet paper and no sweetheart and no Gloria. All of it was gone. So was his life. He had no job. An expensive apartment that he couldn't afford and the only thing he owned was his thirty eight revolver. She had not found it because he had hidden it well away from curious babies.

He wiped his face and Mabel walked over and put her arms around him. She found that she liked this angry young man. He had a bug heart and it was broken.

"We are a lot alike." She told him. "How many people have you held up?"

"You're the first. I kept trying doors where I thought no one was home and yours was the first that opened."

"Where are you living? Where do you sleep?"

"In my car. I have an old Ford that I drive to the

YMCA and shower there and shave. I drive around looking for opportunities. Sometimes people leave change in their pants pockets at the Y and I can get a meal. One time I wandered through a store and a purse sat wide open in the shopping cart and I reached in and took the wallet. That was my biggest haul. I got eighty seven dollars. I also do day labor when I can get it but often when I go there, there's forty fifty guys trying to work and the odds for a black guy are not good. What do you do for money?"

"I am out. Completely. My savings are gone. I have nothing left to sell. I'm completely broke."

"We need to think of something."

She took the meat out of the frying pan and put it with the boiling carrots, potatoes, onions, and celery. He added spices and a little milk. She sat across the table from him and asked, "What could we do to get some money?" She got up and went to the cabinet to grab a can of tomato sauce and added it to the stew mixture. "I'm too chicken to hold up a place and I would probably shoot myself in the foot if I carried a gun." She smiled at him.

"We need a plan for one big one. Enough that we won't have to do it again."

The phone jangled angrily and as Mabel went to answer it, she noticed that Clarence was sitting in her kitchen with his face scrunched up in thought. It was Marie's husband telling Mabel that Marie had survived yet another surgery to remove another lump from her chest. No, it wasn't cancerous but the surgery took a lot out of Marie. He sounded almost sorry that she had not died. Mabel had a difficult time being polite with him. She finally thanked him and hung up. "Bastard."

"Huh?" Clarence looked at her.

"That jackass calls to tell me Marie had another surgery and he sounded pissed that she came through it O.K."

"What does he do for a living?"

"He's into some kind of financial planning. I think."

"Maybe we can get him on the internet" he mused.

"How?" Mabel asked curiously.

"If he's into meeting women on the internet, he didn't quit because his wife got sick. He is just slicker now and we can become the woman of his dreams and before we meet, he has to send us money. That way we have a little cash to work with and then we'll send him lovely, sexy pictures of a gorgeous chick he will kill to go to bed with. Then we blackmail him for 10 grand. If he does not pay right away, we contact him on his jab and scare the daylights out of him. What do you think?"

"I like it, but neither one of us is pretty enough to turn his head." She laughed.

"Don't worry about that. I've got pictures." He grinned. Mabel thought that he had the most teeth she had ever seen on anybody and each one was straight and white against his dark skin.

"The only thing that worries me is that Marie might find out and/or suffer because of it."

"She's not going to find out because the scum has this down pat and you don't believe he stopped because she was ill, do you?"

"No, knowing him. He is as active as ever."

"Do you have his e-mail address?"

"You ready. It's Big Dog in heat. Can you believe it?"

"We'll give him heat that will get so hot his fingers will burn from responding to our girl." He roared.

He told Mabel that he would be back in an hour or so and left, slamming the door behind him and it did not look back again. Mabel shook her head at the whole situation and started to giggle. "What a life, "she thought. "Here I am read it. He deserved whatever he got. The creep.

EXTRACTION

Clarence knocked gently on the door and entered the kitchen, "Wow, it smells great, is it almost done?" He smiled at her a slew of pictures of women in various "Jeez, these women are gorgeous. Where did you get these?" Mabel asked.

"On the internet. They are selling and I wasn't buying; just looking and I downloaded them for the future. Which I guess is here now. Which one do you like best?"

"How much time before the stew is done?"

"About another hour or so."

"Let's do it" They scanned the picture and sent an email to "Big dog" with a note saying that Cheri, the name they chose, would love to meet him but did not have airplane fare to get to him. They sat back and waited for the beep which would tell them that they had a return e-mail. Just as they started eating the beep sounded and they both rushed to the computer to see the message. He had written—"My dreams come true. Mail me the price of the ticket and I will send you the money but come soon. I need you." Love, Maury.

Mabel was furious. "That creep isn't giving Marie a second thought. All he cares about is his own sick needs. Let's get him." Clarence nodded and thought about where the money could go that would not connect them to the scam.

We'll have him write it to a Currency Exchange in my old neighborhood. They just got a new exchange and he'll never know that we are not in Boston like the e-mail says."

They e-mailed him back and asked for $900.00 for the plane fare and a new outfit.

They continued to eat their stew and were just about finished when the beep notified them of an e-mail. The creep had agreed to write the money ASAP and expected Cheri to arrive by the weekend which meant that Marie would still be in the hospital. Clarence left to get the money and Mabel was trying to ask how he would get it without being Cheri. "Don't worry, "he said, "the place I named is crooked and they have been buying food stamps from the poor for years. This is a piece of cake. I'll be back in two hours."

Mabel figured that that was the last she would see of Clarence but he surprised her two and a half hours later. He handed her a huge box of chocolates and grinned with all his teeth. "We have a thousand in cash. Tomorrow we'll go for another thousand. Make some bill payments."

She went into the guest room and cried. Clarence followed her and said, "Look, the guy doesn't deserve your tears."

"Oh, no. That's not why I'm crying. I never expected you to come back." Clarence threw back his head and roared. Pretty soon, they were both on another laughing jag.

"I keep my word, lady." He stated.

"I see. I do too. Here is your room. "No more sleeping in the car. Bring in your clothes and we will work out our arrangement." He smiled and nodded.

He brought in one pathetic little garbage bag which contained all his earthly goods. "You don't know what this means to me. For you to trust me, I mean." He pulled out two pair of jeans and three shirts and assorted personal items. He had a few books and lots of pictures of women. "This." He pointed to the pictures, "is our gold-mine."

"What do we do when he starts suspecting a scam?" Mabel asked.

"We just have responses from other cities, so he doesn't suspect."

"How long can we keep this going?"

"A few months. Long enough for you to pay some bills and have a little in savings."

Then, I'll put some money away and try to find my baby again." He looked so sad that Mabel thought that this is truly a good man. "We also need to keep looking for work." "Yes, I suppose so, but I have had no luck whatsoever."

"We'll keep trying." He reassured her.

"If you could do anything in the world that you wanted, Mabel, what would it be?" He asked contemplatively.

Mabel thought for a moment and responded, "I would sell the house, buy a camper and travel all over the west. I'd eat when I felt like it and sleep when I got tired. I'd drown worms at will and eat what I catch. I'd look at scenery until I got tired of it and stay awake all night if I wanted to. I always wanted to just get up and go." She smiled. "Wow. I like it. Would you take on a partner? Like me? I would love to travel the west and you could tell people that I was your bastard son." He laughed. "I'm pretty good with machines and could fix anything wrong in the camper. I love to fish and we could still go on-line to fleece Maury."

"I could sell the house and car and you could sell your "beater" and we would have enough to live on for a long time. We could clear about forty thousand or so." Mabel stated.

"Let's do it." His enthusiasm was contagious. Mabel thought about it some more and said, "Let's do Maury a bit first and build a little extra. I always wanted to go to Las Vegas and try the slot machines. The money from Maury would fund our trip to

Vegas. If we lose it, no harm and if we win, we're ahead."

"I'll send the sucker another e-mail from the State of Washington." Clarence grinned.

"Let's see how stupid he really is. I'll pick up another blonde."

CHAPTER THREE

They seemed to settle into a pretty good routine. Clarence cut the grass and Mabel trimmed. Clarence bar-b-qued and Mabel ate like a horse. Then, Mabel cooked and Clarence cleaned up. The days were comfortable and calm. Money came rolling in from Maury who had no end to his stupidity. They were five thousand dollars richer and started to look for a camper with two bedrooms that they could drive. One day, driving around Indiana, Clarence yelled, "Stop the car!" She thought that she had lit something but he was smiling as she braked. "Look at that baby." He pointed to a camper sitting next to a farm house, mostly hidden by trees.

They got out of the car and walked around the camper before a man in overalls asked them if they were interested. Clarence wanted to see the inside and Mabel was turned off due to the bird droppings all over the thing.

EXTRACTION

"NO!" She said.

"YES!" He said and they burst out laughing.

The farmer went back into the house to get the key and returned with his wife who was a foot shorter. "Here you go," he said and handed the key to Clarence. Clarence eagerly sprang to the one step and opened it. Mabel reluctantly followed him.

The farmer yelled, "You folks go ahead and check it out. My arthritis is killing me and I'll wait on the porch."

Mabel was astonished that the inside was sparkling clean. The cabinets were in great shape and the floors were spotless.

"Wow." Said Clarence. "This is great and look, it has two bedrooms and a fairly large bathroom. It even has a T.V. and a coffee pot for you. I wonder what he's asking for it?" Mabel was enchanted. The curtains were frilly lace with baby blue cornflowers and the rest of the kitchen matched all the blue. The two couches were blue plaid and in great condition. She poked around while Clarence went to examine the motor. He came back inside and said, "It looks good. Let's try and start her up." The engine kicked over as soon as he turned the key and both looked at each other in surprise.

"I want this." Mabel said.

"Me too."

The farmer was smoking a pipe and asked, "You folks really interested or just looking?"

"How much you want?" asked Clarence?

"Don't rightly know." He answered. "Maybe eight grand."

"All we got is six."

"I could go seven."

"You didn't hear me. All we got is six." Clarence took Mabel's arm to turn away when the farmer said, "Cash?"

"Yes."

"O.K."

"O.K. what?"

"Sold to the huge man." The farmer grinned.

Clarence pulled out his beaten wallet and counted out six thousand in hundreds. "Didn't rob no bank did ya?" asked the farmer.

"Nope. A rich uncle gave it to me." Clarence grinned.

The papers were signed and Clarence drove the camper and Mabel followed him home.

"Okay, what do we do now?" Clarence inquired.

"We could sell the house and travel around the country. Maybe, go to Vegas. Go to Maine and eat lobster. Sit at the side of some lake and drown some worms. Anything we want." She grinned like a schoolgirl.

The house didn't take ling to sell and Mabel and Clarence loaded the camper with clothes and a few treasures they both had acquired.

"Where to first?" he asked.

"Let's just drive and see where we end up. I hate planning."

"Fine with me."

CHAPTER FOUR

"Did you watch the news last night or were you really asleep?" she asked him.

"Guess I dozed off. Why?"

"The newscaster said that people my age are the 'invisible' generation. He said that if we held up a bank, they could not describe us. If we shoplifted, no one would notice." She had a gleam in her eye.

"Oh, no you don't!" He yelled. I'm starting to know you real well and your mind is plotting something."

She grinned and said, "I just want to try and see if it's true."

"NO! NO! and NO!" He roared.

"Sometimes, you're just boring." She announced. "For an armed robber, you have no guts."

"You don't need guts to get killed."

"Nobody shoots an old lady shoplifting."

"There is always a first time and you are the only friend I have in the whole world and I don't want to lose you, dammit."

"OH Clarence, you are so emotional. I'm not going to do anything stupid. I just want to see if it works." She smiled at him.

She went into a Walmart and started poking around the clothes. She took a bra, some undies and a chamois for the RV. She purchased toilet paper and left. She showed Clarence the haul and he grinned. "So, it did work. Eh?"

"Unbelievable. I really don't exist. All the kids they have working there all look like they are sixteen and are busy with each other. The older people employed there seem to be the bean counters and watch the kids. It was really kind of fun."

"You know, if I went in there, everybody would be watching me because I'm Black and big. Security would come out of the woodwork and follow me throughout the store. I have never been in a store without someone watching me."

"OOH, you poor baby." She crackled laughing. "You'll always be Black and big and nothing going to change that."

She made dinner and they sat down to eat when she said, Darn, I meant to send a card to Sonny and let him know that I'm traveling around the country. I don't want him to call the police because he can't get a hold of me."

"Do it first thing tomorrow and tell him he has a brother." He roared and she soon joined the laughter.

"He would die. He is such a prude and lives in white territory. He used to be such a warm giving kid. I just know what happened to him." She stated with tears in her eyes.

Clarence put his arm over her shoulder for a sideway hug and said, "His loss...my gain."

"I love you, big guy." She said. "I don't mean sexually."

"What's wrong with sex?"

"Nothing. That's not what I mean. I love you like a son. I'm not incestuous." She smiled.

"I love you too but I love you like an old friend."

"Are you calling me old?"

"I give up." He laughed, "You know exactly what I mean."

She nodded. "It's bedtime. Tomorrow we'll getup early and go fishing."

He caught a beauty of a catfish. It measured 18" and was fat and around the middle. "Great for lunch. I'll smoke him. I want one more so that you can eat, too." He grinned.

All if her fish were six and seven inches long and ended back in the water.

"I'm going to run into town and be back for lunch. So, you better catch another one." She popped him on the head as she walked by. She washed up and drove to the bank. She would surprise Clarence with a gift. She would put the title of the RV in his name. He would outlive her anyway. She wanted him to have something that he owned and when and if he found his Gloria, three would be a home for her. A man needed a home, she thought, even if it had wheels.

She did no kid herself that she was casing the bank while waiting for the title to be brought back by the red-haired man. Not much on security here, she thought. One lousy camera and on old, old fart of a guy in a wrinkled uniform. He was older than she and tired looking. He was scanning a magazine and seemed disinterested in the surroundings that he was supposed to be watching. "I wonder what he gets paid?"

The red-haired man came back and said, "All set, is there anything else you need, today?" She thanked him and left. She went to the liquor store and bought a bottle of white wine for the celebration she planned. She also went into the grocery store and shoplifted two steaks but purchased side dishes for the fish.

When she went back to the campsite, she could see that Clarence had the smoker going full-blast. She could smell the hickory wood that he liked so much. She peeked under the lid and saw cat fish that were turning golden brown and had been steaked. "Hey, lady, leave the fish alone. We shoot poachers in this here part of the country."

He grinned at her and asked, "Did you get the post-card for Sonny?"

"No, dammit, I forgot. Maybe I'm getting senile. That's what I went into town for, too. Damn. I've got to go back. We've been gone four weeks and Sonny calls at least once a month. Damn."

"But why not eat first?"

"No, the mail goes out at five and it's four thirty now. I also have to buy a card first. Just keep the fish warm for me or wait. It can't take more than thirty minutes. I'll be right back."

CHAPTER FIVE

Clarence looked at his watch for the eighth time in an hour. 6:30 and no RV and no Mabel. He nibbled on the fish and put the rest in the cooler. 7:00 and no mabel. "Damn that woman. Where was she? Did she have an accident? Should he try to walk to town? Should he wait?" All his thoughts were jumbled and he couldn't make a decision. 7:30 and nothing. He started walking towards town at a fast pace. Another camper saw him and offered him a ride. Clarence accepted gratefully and the man drove him to the center of town where there seemed to be a great deal of activity. There were two squad cars, an ambulance and a rescue squad in front of the bank. As Clarence neared the bank, he realized that the RV was parked around the corner without Mabel in it. He went to the entrance of the bank but a young officer held out his arm and told him that he could not go in there. They were bringing out a body on a cart. The body was covered with a large sheet which slipped off the face. It was an old man that had a heart-attack in the lobby and appeared to be dead.

Clarence sighed of relief. "She didn't do anything stupid after all. Whewh. Where the devil was she.?" He walked around the bank and saw no sign of Mabel. He passed a $10.00 haircut place and there was Mabel laughing with a girl that was cutting her hair. Clarence stormed into the beauty parlor and yelled, "What the hell were you thinking?" The entire place was as quiet as a funeral parlor and everyone looked at the giant Black man with fear.

"Stop being grumpy. I'm getting my hair cut for Pete's sake. What is wring with you?"

The beautician had stopped cutting and looked at Mabel with wonder, "You know him?"

"Yes, that's my son."

The proverbial pin could have been heard dropping. The beautiful finished a more snips and Mabel paid and grabbed Clarence by the arm and escorted him out. "What is wrong with you?" You acted like I committed a crime for Crying out loud."

To her surprise, Clarence started crying. Right there in the middle of the sidewalk. At first the tears just streaked down his cheeks but when she hugged him. The sobs came like a little boy's. She couldn't understand a word he was saying but she felt that whatever it was, it had to be serious. Clarence was to "macho" to cry in public. Speaking of public. One dignified gentleman tentatively asked if everything was alright and if there was anything he could do to help. Mabel thanked him and said, "His mother died and he is grieving." She thanked the man for his concern and he went on his way.

Mabel got Clarence into the RV while he blew his nose loud and honking. "My mother died?"

"I don't know what got into you, Clarence. I had to make up something. We were a spectacle."

"I was waiting for you and you didn't come back and the fish was drying out and I didn't know what happened to you and the police were there and they took out a body and I thought that it was you." He finally took a breath and looked at her with watery eyes.

"You thought I was dead?"

"Yes."

"Why would you ever think that?"

"I thought you held up the bank."

"Oh, for crying out loud. Clarence, sometimes you are an idiot...I didn't go into the bank and hold it up. I went in there to get you this. So much for a surprise. Here!" She thrust the papers into his hands and kept driving.

"What's this?"

"Oh, no, I can't take this. It belongs to you. You worked all your life for this."

"Clarence. Shut up. Let's get a meal. I'm starving."

CHAPTER SIX

They were in Texas. A small town right outside Amarillo. Clarence had been napping and Mabel was stretching her left arm and then her right. Clarence looked at her and asked, "Are you tired?"

"Yes, it's my turn to nap. But I think we should eat first. Somebody told me this restaurant in Armarillo were you can get a 72 ounce steak and if you eat it all, it's free. I bet you could do it."

She parked the RV in the second designated for it and they entered the restaurant. A seven foot bear stood at the register and loomed over them. The place had ambiance. There were critters that neither recognized and they were all stuffed and hanging from the ceiling and some were mounted on the walls. She hoped that the meat they were ordering was not on of them. They stood and waited to be seated, like the sign said. Everyone else was seated except them. Clarence whispered, "There are no blacks in here, did you notice?"

"So?"

"That's why we're standing here instead of sitting."

Mabel could feel herself getting angry. She looked at her watch and realized that they had been standing for thirty minutes. The place was not crowded. She was getting furious, now. "I want to speak to the manger!" She yelled.

A waitress tried to hush her but Mabel was beyond hushing and repeated herself even louder. A tiny little man with a one hair comb-over appeared from the kitchen area. He was wringing his hands and could not make eye contact with either of them.

"Why are we still standing here, Mister?" Mabel demanded.

He stuttered and tried to tell them they were busy and would have to wait to be seated. Mabel looked at the room and counted fourteen empty tables. We can sit at any of those tables that are empty. "What are we waiting for? He is not going to turn white if that's what you're thinking. He will forever be Black. Now, what's the deal here?"

He stuttered some more and complained about kitchen help and the waitress shortage.

Mabel looked at the little weasel and said, "If we

don't get seated within the next thirty seconds, I will call the ACLU and Jesse Jackson and you will have a circus out here that you won't believe. This Black gentleman here works for the FBI and I will have the Health Department down on you throat so far that you'll sprout hair. In fact, the IRS will be contacted, too. Now, seat us."

As he led the way to a nice corner table, the customers in the place applauded Mabel's speech. "Right on, Mama." Said a young man with his wife and kids. "He forgot that this is the United States of America and we all have rights. I served with my Black brothers in Iraq and wouldn't be here if one had not pulled me for more than a mile through rubble and bombing. Yea, lady. You're the man." He got up and shook both of their hands. They thanked him and sat down.

The waitress was very pleasant and apologized for her boss and Mabel told her that no one could apologize for someone else's behavior and all people were responsible for their actions. Their food arrived shortly and Clarence made small work of the 72 ounce steak. The owner came out and congratulated him but did not shake his hand. Mabel was angry again but decided to swallow it. He comped their meal and seemed glad to see them go.

"Now there's someone I could rob and lose no sleep over." Mabel told him on the way to the RV. "I would mess up the place just to give him a message."

"Let it go, Mabel. It's not worth it. It's happening all over. All the time."

"That doesn't make it right."

"No, it doesn't."

"Where to Clarence? I don't like it here."

"How about Vegas? You ever been there?"

"A long time ago. After my divorce. I went with an old boyfriend. Let me tell you about life's most embarrassing moment. He was a sexual freak and always wanted to try something different. So, we were in the hotel and he brings out baby oil. Said that he saw it on a TV show. He heated it in the microwave and proceeded to smear it all over me. Then he says, "It's your turn. Do me." I play along an slather it all over him. I lay down and he jumps on top of me and lo behold, he slides right off into the end table and knocks himself out. I call 911 and hurridly get dressed. He is buck naked and out cold, bleeding from the head. The EMTs arrive and ask what happened. I couldn't tell them. They get out smelling salts and slap a bandage on his head. He groans and comes to. They ask what happened and he says, 'I can't tell you guys,' They have to write a report and don't know what to put in it. I tell them just put in there that he tripped and hit his head. They nod gratefully and leave. No sex that night because every time I tried I burst out laughing. We broke up after we came home. But I'll never forget that night."

Clarence was wiping his eyes and making motions with his one hand flying over the other. He kept laughing and visualizing the scene over and over.

She said, "Tell me a funny story, now."

"The only one I can think of if the edible panties."

"The what?"

"Edible panties. They were red licorice and made into bikini pants. The woman would wear them and the guy would try to eat them off of her. So, we were in my apartment and she had them on. She coaxed me to come eat them. I dived right in and ate the whole thing and next thing you know, I'm in the emergency room. In anaphtlaactic shock. I was allergic to the stuff. They cut off my watch and ring and put a tube down me throat. Then they asked me what I had eaten. I told them licorice and she told them edible panties. A tour of the hospital employees came to look at me. I felt like a freak.

Everything was swollen with hives. I itched like crazy and everyone was laughing at the dope that ate the panties."

"That's almost as bad as the baby oil."

"Yeah, I know."

Mabel was cracking up. She thought that she was the only one to do stupid things but she was wrong. It was nice to know that others did dumb things, too.

"According to the map, we are only an hour from Vegas now. Shall we look and see what kind of camping they have there? Pull over."

Clarence eased the RV on to the shoulder and she showed him the campground map. "I like the one near the dam. I can fish when we get tired of giving them money. How much do we have left, anyway?"

"We're O.K. for a while but we need to come up with a new way to get some big bucks. This won't last forever."

"I can work. I'm strong."

"We'll see. We're fine for now. Maybe we'll hit a jackpot."

"Yeah, right but don't hold your breath."

CHAPTER SEVEN

She had been at this machine for the whole night. Clarence had gone to sleep at around one in the morning but she felt a steak coming. The machine kept playing around with 2 sevens and the third was a line above or below. It was coming. She knew it. She had to pee but didn't want to leave the machine. Finally, a floor walker came over and she asked him to not let anyone else play her machine. He told her to hurry. She went to the washroom and bought a ham sandwich from a vendor. Drinks were free. She went back and put in more silver dollars. She turned to wave a waitress over and heard the clanking of the Pavlovian draw. Her machine was paying. Paying! Paying! Paying! Twenty-five thousands worth. Security came over with paper work and told her that the machine only pays one thousand and the rest would be given to her in cash. She that Uncle Sam wanted his cut off her winnings. Security reset the machine and handed her a check for 24,000 dollars. She decided to play only $500 more. She dropped in the three coins and watched the sevens play with her. She saw Clarence looking groggy make his way through the casino. The check was in her pocket and the five trays of coins sat at the side of the machine. She smiled at him and dropped three more coins into the slot. Round and round and damn, there they were. Three sevens on the same line. He jumped up and down like a little boy and told her that she won. The payoff was $5,000. Here came the same security man again.

"WOW, lady. You're killing us." He smiled. He reset the machine and went to get her a check.

"Lobster tonight, woman. You buy. I want to eat in style. I might even have a steak with it. Champagne and strawberries with whipped cream."

"You're on. That sounds great. We'll have to get dressed up for this."

"Naw. This is Vegas. As long as you can pay, they don't care what we wear."

She threw $600 more into the machine but it was done paying. "I need to sleep first. hen we'll go eat O.K.?"

"Sure, I'll drown some worms."

CHAPTER EIGHT

She awoke around six and headed for the shower. God, she was hooked on that machine. Hadn't slept in two days. Starving. She scrubbed her hair and combed it out into a soft fluff. She put on black shades and a red silk blouse.

Clarence walked into the camper just as she was getting ready to leave.

"Give me five minutes and I'll be ready, too. Wow. You look great."

He jumped into the shower and the water soon turned cold, "AAARRRGGGGHHH."

She started laughing. He had done it to her three days ago. One forgets that the water heater in a camper is much smaller than one in a house. True to his word, he was ready in five minutes. Clean gray slacks and a light blue shirt. His hair was neatly brushed and he offered his arm. They sauntered towards Caesar's Palace where she had made reservations for seven.

They arrived promptly and were immediately seated in a semi-circle of a bench. The table was pushed in front of them. A half-dressed female introduced herself to Clarence as his "slave girl" and a young boy with only a loin cloth was Mabel's "slave boy." The first course was an appetizer of unknown origin. She tasted it but did not like it. Clarence ate it all. Then came the soup. Then the lobster in butter. The steak cooked to perfection. The salad. Each course accompanied by champagne. On and on fifteen courses later came the strawberry sundae with giant strawberries and whipped cream. She ate one strawberry and looked longingly at what she could not eat. She felt drunk. Was it the overstuffed belly of the champagne? She could hardly move. A discreet tab was given to her and she placed her credit card beneath the leather flap with Caesar's insignia on it. She had never had a $300.00 meal before and left a substantial tip. She felt as if she could go without food for a whole week now. Clarence put his hand to his mouth to stifle one of his famous burps.

"God, I'm full."

"Me too."

"Will it help?"

He laughed and helped her up. The "slave girl" whispered in her ear and Mabel started laughing.

When they got outside, Clarence asked what the whispering was about. "She thinks I'm smart for having a young stud like you to take care of me." They both laughed and realized that people did not understand their relationship.

As they walked, Mabel told Clarence how much she had won today. He stopped in his tracks and picked her up and swung her around. "My Lord, I never thought that it was that much. We have a breather now." Suddenly he looked depressed.

"What is it? What's bothering you?"

"Nothing."

"Bull."

He was quiet for a long time. Mabel figured that he would tell her when he was ready.

"I feel like a kept man."

"Really."

"You give me the RV. You win the money. You buy the food. You even buy the worms. What do I contribute?"

"Friendship. No price on that. I can't ever remember having a wonderful friend like you. No sex, no confusion. Just real people being real friends. No clouding of the issues. We talk. We tell each other secrets. I have never been friends with a man without a sexual overtone. This is a hell of a lot better. We know who we are and what we want. We are so much alike that sometimes it scares me. I know you need to get some nookie soon. I ca see the frustration building up in you. Go. Get some. I'll be home when you're done."

He leaned over and gently kissed her cheek. "I love you."

She made her way to the RV looking forward to more sleep. She wished Clarence luck in connecting tonight. He was a good man.

CHAPTER NINE

She heard banging. She awoke with a start wondering what the noise was and what they were doing. She pulled on her robe and went to the coffee pot and turned it on. The banging started again and she realized that someone was banging on her door. She opened it and two men in suits stood there. "Are you Mabel? Do you know a Clarence Carter?"

"What happened? Is he okay? Who are you?" Mabel was not awake yet but knew whatever they had to tell her was not good.

The fat one pulled out a wallet and introduced himself. His shiny badge reflected the sun and hurt her eyes.

"Detective Martin and this is Detective Barnes. Sex crimes."

"What? Sex crimes?"

"Yes, ma'am. May we come in?" He was very polite.

She went to the coffee pot and poured herself a cup and stirred in the creamer. "Do you want some coffee?"

"Yes, ma'am, if it's no trouble. Black please and cream for him."

Mabel poured two more cups and set the cream and spoons in front of them.

"How are you related to Mr. Carter?"

"He's my son." She said with a straight face.

"I see. Where were you last night around midnight?"

"Here, sound asleep."

"Where was Carter?" Should she tell him that he went looking to get laid or just make something up.

"I think he went to gamble. I'm not sure. I was tired and he was wide awake and not ready to sleep. I left him on the strip after we had eaten."

"What time was that?"

"Maybe around ten. I really didn't notice the time. We sat to eat at seven and the meal took about two and a half hours. What is this all about. Where is Clarence?"

"He's in lock-up. A young lady accused him of rape."

"No way! Clarence is not a rapist."

"That's for the judge to decide."

"Has he had a bail hearing?"

"He is up for arraignment in two hours or so. Then bail will be set. We can take you to see him."

"Let me throw on some clothes and comb my hair. Give me a minute."

They drove to the outskirt of the strip in silence. Mabel wondering what had happened. They arrived at the station at 9:30 and the desk officer nodded down the hall. Mabel moved in the direction of the cell and drunk yelled, "Hey baby do me first." Mabel shot him a dirty look and he shut up and sat down on the bunk.

Clarence looked up with red eyes and said, "Mabel, I did not do this. I did not rape her."

"What did you do after I left you?"

"I went into Caeser's and had a drink in the jazz bar. I was listening and felt a tap on my shoulder. I turned around and there she stood. The "slave girl" that served me the food. She said 'Hi studly. Remember me?' I guess I grinned and offered to buy her a drink even though she looked like she already had a few before I got there. Then she wanted to know where my 'sugar mama' was and she started rubbing my thigh. I told her that you were not my 'sugar mama' but rather a friend. She started laughing and saying that she could be my friend but that I would have to 'put out.' She said it had been a long time since she had dark meat and was I interested. Oh, yeah. I told her. Where do you want to go? She said she had a room at Caeser's and we could go there. Her room was on the fourth floor and we were hot and heavy into it when a guy hit me upside my head. She screamed and called him a bastard. He slapped her a couple of times and called her a whore. I kind of exploded and knocked the guy out with one punch to the jaw. Next thing I know, I'm under arrest for rape."

"I remember her and her smart remark when we were leaving the dining room. She was looking to shake you down, that's all. Go wash your face. You're due in court in five minutes."

The judge was a silver-haired, middle aged white man. He had a no nonsense look about him. He asked Clarence if he had an attorney. Clarence shook his head and the judge said, "Mr. Carter you need to answer verbally so that the clerk can record it."

"No sir, I don't have an attorney."

"We can appoint one or you can get one of your choice. Bail is set for $100,000. Next case."

The bailiff was going to escort Clarence back to the cell when Mabel spoke up. "How much is that for cash?"

EXTRACTION

"Ten thousand, lady. Pay the clerk and bring me the receipt and he can go." Nodding to Clarence who was handcuffed and looking defeated.

Mabel opened her purse and the shocked clerk helped her count out $10,000. "Hurry with the receipt please. I need to get him out."

"Your boyfriend?" the clerk asked.

"No, my son." The clerk looked speechless and handed her the receipt. Mabel rushed to the lock-up and Clarence was freed. He hugged her and thanked her repeatedly.

When they got outside Clarence said, "You know that they'll find me guilty, don't you?"

"No they won't. Let's find a lawyer. A good one."

"How?"

"I'll know when I see him."

CHAPTER TEN

The first lawyer had on a brown suit with black shoes. Mabel nixed him. The second lawyer had a hair piece, a bad one. Mabel nixed him and muttered something about not trusting a man with a wig. It looked like it was made from cat hair. The third had on white socks with a black pair of pants. The fourth one had cheap shoes which had never seen polish. The fifth one was a woman who wore a smart grey suit with a spotless white blouse. Her heels were sensible and her hair was pulled back in a French twist.

"This is the one," Mabel told Clarence. They explained everything to her and she nodded and took notes. She asked many questions and when she seemed satisfied she leaned back and said, "I'll take the case. $20,000 up front and more if I need to hire an investigator."

Mabel agreed that that was fair and she signed

papers for the fee. Mabel asked for the nearest ATM and said she would return shortly. Mabel dropped $20,000 on the lawyer's desk and asked for a receipt. She pulled out a receipt book and proceeded to write. "I need a phone number so that I can reach you for the court date." Mabel gave her the cell phone number and they left.

They decided to walk back to the RV instead of hailing a cab.

"I'm sorry, Mabel. I should have gone home with you. I was selfish last night. I sure as hell should not have taken on a white girl. Jesus, I am stupid."

"Shut your mouth, Clarence. This is not your fault. Stop beating yourself up over what someone else did. The girl was trying to shake you down, that's all. She thought you had money because we ate there. Only rich people eat there. She thought she had Christmas when she saw you at the bar."

"My hormones got the best of me."

"Yeah."

Trail was set for two weeks from tomorrow at nine a.m. Clarence was convinced that he would get twenty years and no amount of consoling was working. He was jumpy and irritable for the two weeks. He went for walks around the campsite and sat by the water fishing with no bait. He had lost a great deal of weight and pushed his food around the plate. Mabel saw nothing go into his mouth.

"Enough, Clarence. We have a good lawyer and you will win this. Now, stop acting like a three year old and shove some food into your mouth before I feed you."

He actually grinned at her and ate slowly and sparingly. All she cared about was that he ate something.

Clarence was up at five and she could hear the shower running. "He didn't fall asleep at all," she thought. She groaned as she swung her feet to the floor. Coffee. That's the answer.

He came out of the bathroom with a pin-stripe navy blue suit and three ties. The pale blue shirt screamed for a maroon or college stripe tie. She grabbed one out of his closet and handed it to him. His shoes were glossy and he smelled of expensive after-shave.

"You look good." She told him with approval. "But court doesn't start for four more hours. You gonna sit in the steps?"

She poured him a cup of coffee and he drank it slowly. "I guess I'm nervous. Never been on trial before."

EXTRACTION

"I won't let anything happen to you. You know that, right?"

"Mabel, I don't want to hurt your feelings but I think this is beyond your control. My life is going down the drain and somebody else pulled the plug. A liar and a con. How so we fight that with truth?"

"There are many different ways to get to the truth. This floozy is not going to win. Hear?"

She sounded so sure of herself that he actually started to relax a bit. Maybe the girl would tell the truth, after all. There is always hope.

CHAPTER ELEVEN

The "slave girl" was barley recognizable in a demure navy blue suit with a white blouse. Her hair was pulled back into a French twist and she wore very thin earrings. Her make-up was minimal, unlike the slave girl look with lots of thick eye make up and dangling silver chains from her ears. Her heels were tasteful and downplayed her good looks.

Miss Warren had just called the "slave girl" to the stand. She was sworn in and Miss Warren asked why they were in her room at the hotel. The girl stated that they were just talking and wanted privacy. Miss Warren asked if she always talked with her clothes off. People snickered and the judge asked for silence from the spectators.

"Tell the court why your clothes were off and you were just talking?" persisted Miss Warren.

"UHM, we were getting comfortable."

"You agreed to become naked?"

"Well, he ripped my clothes off so he could have sex with me." She said while looking at her boyfriend who was sitting four rows away from the prosecuting table. He looked smug.

"Are these the clothes you were wearing that evening?" asked Miss Warren holding up a black shirt and gold blouse.

"Yes."

"They don't look torn to me."

"Objection, your honor, counsel is making a statement!" The District attorney yelled.

"Sustained. Please ask a question Miss Warren. "The white-haired judge was frowning at her.

"Show me where the clothes are torn." She handed the items to the "slave girl."

The girl took them and finally found a seam that had opened up in the rear of the pants.

"Here," she said triumphantly pointing to the small tear in the seat of the pants.

"This little rip is what you claim my client did in order to rape you?"

"Yes. He was very strong."

"Did he do anything else to you?"

"Well," she hesitated, "he ripped my clothes off and proceeded to rape me."

"Miss Corsi, please tell the court how many times

you have sat here and accused someone of raping you?" Miss Warren shot at her.

The girl turned pale and the D.A. jumped up and objected. The judge denied the objection and the girl looked towards the boyfriend for help.

"Please answer the question, Miss Corsi." Miss Warren urged.

The boyfriend was shaking his head and Miss Corsi answered, "Never."

"Your honor," Miss Warren addressed the judge, "I have here four previous accusations of rape by Miss Corsi. I want to admit this into evidence and file a contempt of court charge."

The judge reached for the police reports and scanned them quickly and then frowned at Miss Corsi. "I would like an explanation of this young lady. You were sworn in and promised to tell the truth. Now, I see that you blatantly lied to this court. We will have a thirty minute recess and then you will explain this to the court." He banged his gavel and the room emptied out. Miss Warren, Clarence and Mabel were the only ones left.

Mabel immediately understood what was happening. "You have proved her to be a liar. Does that mean Clarence will be free?"

"It depends on the judge and how he will view

EXTRACTION

this. Let's get a cup of bad coffee in the cafeteria."

They drank the coffee and looked around the room. "There they are," Miss Warren pointed across the room at the "slave girl" and the D.A. "The D.A. does not look happy with her. He hates to lose." Miss Warren smiled.

"I did not rape her." Clarence said. "She was more than willing until her boyfriend got there and then she yelled rape. But the funny thing was that he hit her after her hit me. He called her a 'whore' and would have kept hitting her if I hadn't punched him."

"Your guilt or innocence is not a question here." Miss Warren replied.

"What do you mean?"

"The issue here is whether or not she is a liar. I have proof that she is and that lets you off the hook. The clothes are in tact and she has a history of crying rape. Let's go back."

They walked up a flight of stairs and entered the courtroom. "All rise." The bailiff yelled.

"Miss Corsi you are still under oath and will resume the stand. Do you understand that I can send you to jail for perjury?"

"Yes, your honor."

"I will rule later. Counselor resume your questioning."

Miss Warren rose and stood in front of Miss Corsi's view of the boyfriend. "Miss Corsi, isn't it true that you have accused four men of raping you prior to this time?"

"Yes." She whispered.

"You need to speak up, Miss Corsi." The judge declared.

"Yes."

"Isn't it true that you and your boyfriend shake down diners form the Bacchanal room?"

"Objection your honor. Miss Warren is asking Miss Corsi to incriminate herself." The D.A. was red in the face and looked very uncomfortable about this case.

"Overruled."

"Answer the question, Miss Corsi. Aren't all your victims previous diners?"

"Yes."

"Isn't it true that you lure them to your room and then the boyfriend walks in and acts outraged?"

"Yes."

"Your honor, we ask the court to dismiss the charges against Mr. Carter and institute charges of perjury against Miss Corsi."

The judge looked at Clarence and a hint of a smile was seen around the corner of his lips and he banged the gavel, "Case dismissed! Miss Corsi and Mr. Feldman in my chambers please. The D.A. shook his head like a sparring partner in a boxing ring and rose and escorted Miss Corsi to the judge's chamber.

Mabel hugged Miss Warren and then grabbed Clarence and hugged him. He looked bewildered and lost. "It's all over."

"It's time to leave Vegas," Mabel whispered to him.

CHAPTER TWELVE

They arrived in Utah early the next morning. The sign said, "Morton Salt."

Mabel said, "Did you know that all the salt in the world comes from right here?" She pointed to the vastness of the desert and pointed out the contrast of the black mountains and the pure white sand. The sun was just rising and the reflection on the sand hurt their eyes. "Do you want to stop?"

"I would."

They got out the camper and walked across the sand to the water also thick with salt. Their feet were crunching with every step as the salt broke on top of the sand. The mountains loomed and the black also reflected the sun.

"We need better eye protection. This could blind us. This is penetratingly harsh.

Grab me a hat, please.

Clarence ran back to the side of the road and

jumped into the camper. He came back with two hats and asked which one she wanted. She took his fishing hat and crammed it down to her eyebrows. He took the baseball cap and put it on.

"That's a lot better."

They walked hesitatingly into the water and still could hear the salt breaking. Mabel reached down and touched the water and tasted it. "Pure salt." He tasted it too and spit it out.

We need to find a place for breakfast and then a campsite where we can relax.

They were sitting in lawn chairs by the water. Each was watching their lines for a hint of a hit. "I love you, Mabel. There has never been anyone in my life like you."

"The feeling is mutual. We are special together."

"You spend all the money you won on me. What is I had raped her?"

"I know that you are not capable of something like that. You're one of those 'good guys.'"

"How do you know that I'm not capable? Don't we all have the capabilities of evil?"

"I would say that most people do but not you."

"Why not me?"

"Some people are reactionary and impulsive and you are a plotter."

"A what?"

"A person who plots out everything. You have a conscience that rules your behavior."

"I'm more than capable of a spontaneous act than you are because the consequences don't matter to me."

"Don't I matter to you?"

"Very much but you missed the point."

"The point is...?"

"You had a gun, but you couldn't use it. Even though you were desperate. It is not in you."

"I would shoot you and not look back."

"Come on, I don't think that you have the kind of heart, Mabel."

"Then you don't know me. I have shot someone in the butt once when I was working security at a store. I also beat the hell out of an inmate when he stacked me in the tunnel of the jail."

"What?"

"I was assigned to work a crew and this one inmate snuck up behind me and put his forearm across my throat and I threw him against the wall of the tunnel and broke his back."

"My god woman! I had no idea that you were capable of violence like that."

"We all are under the right circumstances. If your

Gloria was threatened what would you be capable of doing to save her?"

"I would do anything to save her."

"Including committing murder?"

"Yes, I guess so."

"You don't know? You guess? You don't know yourself, Clarence."

"I know me."

"No, you don't. If you were a killer, you would have killed me the day you came into my house without all that talking. You would have shot me and left me bleeding while you searched for goodies to take. Clarence, you're full of shit."

"Mabel, you are about to piss me off. If I kill someone do you want me drag their body in front of you for proof?"

Mabel couldn't resist a small snicker and said, "Hey, look at your line. You've got something."

The pole started to move through the grass towards the water and Clarence jumped up to grab it. He started to reel it in and felt a tug at the end. The pole looked as though it would snap in half. Clarence struggled and started sweating. "What the hell have I got here? Maybe a whale." He was laughing and the tension from the conversation was broken as Mabel joined him at the edge of the water.

"It's a big one, whatever it is."

He reeled a few more times and the pole seemed to be getting heavier and heavier. Finally, something broke through the water. "It's a foot!" Clarence bellowed.

"Cut the line. Now." Mabel ordered. "We're leaving."

CHAPTER THIRTEEN

"We are going to drive until we find a town that appears to be sane. We don't need anymore problems. Could you see what would have happened if we had reported a body in the water. We'd both be locked up and they would throw away the keys."

"Mabel, how much money do we have left?"

"Not one hell of a lot. But we will be O.K. I want to buy a small car that we could tow."

"What do we need a car for?"

"We could save a lot of money by leaving the camper at the site and driving around in a small car. The gas we would save would help a lot."

"Not a bad idea. I'll help you look for one."

They had to buy a tow bar for the car they bought and had it attached at the dealership. The car was a beige Neon. A very non-descript car. It had only 60,000 miles on it and it ran fine. Mabel liked the fact that it wasn't flashy.

"So, how come we don't do it? " Clarence asked her.

"Do what?"

"A little poontang."

"I'm old enough to be your mother for God's sake."

"If you were a movie star, you would want a young stud, though."

"If I were a movie star, I wouldn't know you."

"Got a point there. But a little nookie wouldn't hurt. Would it?"

"Clarence! We are friends and when friends become lovers they lose the friendship. Then they worry about cheating and pleasing and losing sleep. The whole flavor changes and that's not what I want. If you want sex it will have to be with someone else, not me. I love you, Clarence but not like that. Now we will never discuss this again. Promise?"

"Nope. I'll wear you down."

"Let's go get some lunch." She jumped up and handed him the car keys. He drove slowly and carefully to an old barn that had been concerted to a restaurant. They ordered a large meal of beef stew, salad, bread and colas. They munched incomplete silence. The waitress kept looking at them for some sign. Were they lovers? Were they family? Were they friends? The odd couple. She waited to give them the bill and smiled graciously as Clarence left a large tip.

They explored the town and looked in the window of an antique store, a beauty parlor and the local bar. The town was about six square city blocks. Some mothers with small children were strolling down the sidewalk oblivious to their surroundings. A few elderly men sat on a bench outside the barber shop and eyed all the women going pass them. A lonely mongrel, which looked like it hadn't eaten in a week, searched for food around the garbage cans and Mabel called it and hunched down to try to pet it. The dog licked her hand and she was hooked. "Go buy me a couple of plain burgers." She said to Clarence. He came back with a greasy bag and handed it to her. She offered it to the dog and he wolfed it down in two bites. She broke the other burger into smaller pieces and hand-fed the dog. "He needs water, too. Would you mind?" Clarence came back with a cup full of water and the dog drank greedily. After the dog finished both burgers and the water, it looked at her and let out a loud burp.

"He sounds like you after a big meal." They

laughed at the animal.

They continued their walk and the dog stayed a couple of paces behind them.

"We are going to keep him." She declared. The dog jumped into the car with them and she slowly drove around a large shopping mall just outside the town limits. There was a bank, beauty shop, hardware store, coffee shop and a Walmart. Mabel parked in front of the Walmart and went in to buy a couple of things for the dog. Her bill came to $42.67. She had flea soap, two dishes, a brush, heart worm medicine and a doggie bed and a couple of different foods and treats for the dog.

Clarence laughed at her lugging the items to the car. "Good grief, woman, this is a dog, not a child. He doesn't need all those things."

"Shut up, Clarence."

They both were laughing by now when Clarence said, "What the world are we going to do with this mangy mutt? He might have a home and just took off. We don't want to steal some little kid's dog."

"If he had a home, he wouldn't look so pathetic, would he?"

"I guess not."

They got to the campsite and took the dog into the laundry area and put him in a wash tub. Mabel scrubbed the dog clean and reassured him the whole time he was being washed. "He's such a good boy. He just wants to be clean and live with us. Doesn't he?"

Clarence wondered if she was waiting for the dog to answer her. Mabel really seemed to like the little mutt and he did seem pretty well behaved. He helped Mabel dry the dog and the dog actually sat still while she brushed his hair. When she was done, she looked at him over and said, "You're almost cute, you know that?" The dog licked her cheek and she giggled like a school girl. She cuddled him and rubbed him behind his ear. "I guess we need to give him a name."

"Rover."

"No way."

"Skip. He looks like that dog in the movie."

"Not bad. But not creative enough."

"Buster."

"I like it. Buster it is. Come Buster."

The dog wagged his tail and got up and walked over to Mabel.

"I don't believe this. This dog is either super-bright or this is just a fluke. Clarence, stand on the other side of the room and call him and we'll see if he is bright."

The dog passed the test and they decided to try the experiment outside and see if the dog would obey. Again, the dog passed with flying colors.

"We have a smart animal here," Clarence begrudgingly announced. He really didn't want to like the dog but had to admit that if they were going to have one, they couldn't have picked a better one. "Let's try a couple of things with him. I'll go walk over to that tree and you tell him to stay. Then, let him loose and tell him to 'find me." Clarence started to walk away and the dog was right behind him.

"This isn't going to work." Mabel said. "Stay Buster!"

The dog promptly sat and looked at her. Clarence had walked a couple of hundred yards to a large Oak tree and he hid behind it.

"Find!" Mabel ordered. The dog sat and looked at her. She repeated the order but the dog did not move. "This isn't working, Clarence," she yelled.

"Come, Buster." Yelled Clarence back and the dog took off like the proverbial bat out of hell and ran straight to Clarence.

"We are doing something wrong, not the dog. There has to be a release order after we order him to stay or something. We didn't get it right."

"Let's go back to the campsite and feed him and

us. We'll try again later. Buster happily loped behind them and jumped into the back seat of the car like he belonged there. They drove back to the camp and fed the dog. The dog burped again after his meal and they both laughed. Mabel place the cushion for the dog bed in the corner of the living room and Buster circled it twice and plopped down on it, letting out a long sigh.

"We need to get him tags so that we don't get into trouble with the law," Clarence stated.

"This is a really good dog and maybe I'll spend some time training him and see what he can do. This dog has been trained and someone is probably looking for him."

"You know, I can understand people hurting each other because they have a tendency to get on each other's nerves but I have never understood someone hurting an animal. I would bet you that campers just left him in town because they didn't want to be bothered anymore hoping that he would be run over. I've seen people let their dogs out on the expressway for that. This I don't understand. If someone could not keep up with Buster, then they deserve to lose him. At least I know that we'll take good care of him and feed him, take him to the vet and whatever else he needs. He'll be safe with us. He can go with us wherever we go and probably won't be too much trouble. I'm getting rather fond of the little thing. Look how tiny he really is all curled up in his bed. He just seems to fit into our eclectic family."

"You gotta promise not to pick up anymore strays, Mabel. Buster and me are enough. I don't want to share you with anything else. I even think I'm jealous of the damn dog. Boy, I am losing what little mind I had."

"You're first with me Clarence. Don't worry. Didn't you ever hear the saying that a mother's heart is big enough to love a dozen kids?"

"I'm not your kid Mabel. I want to be more than that but you won't let me. I could really show you what a real family is all about."

"I have been there and done that and so have you. I make a lousy wife. I love my independence and freedom. I don't want a husband, lover or boyfriend. You need to get off this topic and give it a rest."

"If we just tried it once, maybe you would like it."

"I've had more sex in my lifetime than I wish to remember. I've had good sex, bad sex and just so-so sex. You would fit into one of those categories and then the relationship we have cannot be retrieved. I've once screwed up a really decent friendship by insisting on having sex and that was the end of the friendship because he was lousy at it and I said something about his lack of skills. I've had one night stands, live-in boyfriends, husbands and occasional fuck buddies. I am through with emotional turmoil. Through. Do you hear me?"

"OK, OK, I won't bring it up again. But I do love you."

The dog stood at the door and let out one soft, "Woof." Mabel opened the door and Buster ran out and sprayed the nearest tree and then ran in a circle and did his business. He ran back to the trailer and sat her feet. She gave him a biscuit and he took it to his bed and placed it under the cushion. She gave him another one and he did the same thing.

"I wonder what that is all about?" She asked Clarence. "I've never seen a dog do that. Usually they wolf the treat down."

"I don't know but I have a feeling there are a lot of things we'll learn about Buster."

CHAPTER FOURTEEN

"What do you mean 'What do I think I'm doing? I'm a grown woman who raised you and I know exactly what I want to do." She was getting exasperated trying to explain to Sonny that she was living the life she chose.

"I really don't care what people think I'm not senile and I've reached the age where I feel that I do things without having to explain to people or ask permission."

Sonny retorted that he had called the police to go check on her when they found a young couple living there and he didn't know where she had gone. He told her that he was worried, that's all.

"You're right. I should have let you know sooner than now. I owed you that." She agreed. She could not stand his voice almost whining like he was six and didn't get his way with his toys. Clarence was sitting there grinning at her side of the conversation.

"Okay, Sonny, I'm senile and just trying my wings. No, you don't have to worry about my safety. I have a large body-guard that's traveling with me."

"No, not B_A_C_K, B_L_A_C_K as in colored. I don't care. This is 2006 and to reiterate, I'm grown." She sighed impatiently, "Okay, I'll some and live with you. I'll let you take care of me and buy my clothes and food. God, doesn't that sound like fun?" She could hear him whispering to his wife that she was traveling with a black man. She smirked a little at how horrified he must be. She winked at Clarence and went back to the conversation.

"Why are we discussing this, anyway? I will do what I want and live the way I want. When we decide to drive down South, we'll stop for a visit. I really don't wish to discuss this anymore. Bye." She hung up abruptly and turned to Clarence and said, "I can't believe his nerve. He doesn't call me to see if I'm O.K. but he wants to critique what I do."

"Give the guy a break, Mabel. He might truly have been worried when he couldn't get a hold of you and then the police tell him that you don't live there anymore. That had to be quite a shock."

"I guess but it's the way he says things."

"Mabel, he's your son."

"He frustrates me. It's like he wants me to live the

way he expects and not even consider what I want. Where was he when I needed something? He is too cheap and too controlling."

"Mabel, I really think you're overreacting to him."

"I need to let him go."

"What do you mean?"

"I need to stop trying to be a mother to him and just treat him as someone that I once knew."

"I feel bad for you. He does sound like a self-inflated jerk."

"Yep. Let's go play with the dog."

They took Buster outside and Clarence threw the ball as far as he could and Buster took off after it. He raced back and dropped it at Clarence's feet. "Good boy!" Clarence reached down and petted him. He threw it a few more times and then said,

"Keep him here, Mabel. I'm going to hide the ball and see if he can find." Mabel sat in the grass and scratched the dog's ears and the dog rolled over and offered his stomach to her. She rubbed his stomach and Buster seemed to sigh with delight. Clarence was almost out of sight when he called for Buster. Buster ran to Clarence and she could hear him say, "Find the ball." The dog sniffed the ground for a while and after a few minutes unearthed the ball and dropped it at his feet.

EXTRACTION

"Mabel, you've got to see this. It's unbelievable. This dog is trained to find things. We need to go for a ride and one of us step out of the car at one spot and the other drive further and then let the dog out and see if he can find people. Do you want to stay and I'll drive with the dog?"

They agreed to go further into the country to see if it would work. Mabel stepped out of the car and Clarence continued on his way with the dog for about a mile. He opened the car door and told Buster, "Go find Mabel." The dog raced off and Clarence followed him in the car. Buster seemed to hesitate for a second and took off with his ears pinned back. Mabel was sitting behind a tree when Buster jumped into her lap and rolled onto his back. She scratched his stomach and the dog seemed to be dozing when Clarence pulled up and said. "Incredible. Just incredible. I clocked a whole mile and he still found you. I wonder if he was a Police dog or an Army dog. I still am amazed that he is not with his family. How could he get lost?"

"I don't know and I don't care. He's mine now and I'm not giving him up." They played a few more ball games with the dog and finally decided that they were hungry.

"I'll cook tonight." Clarence announced. "How

about a couple of T-bones and baked potato and salad?"

"Sounds great. Let's go."

As soon as the car door opened, Buster jumped into the back seat and curled up in a ball. Mabel put his food in the dish and refreshed the dog's water. Buster ate greedily and let out his grateful burp and proceeded to his bed and instantly went to sleep.

"How do our finances look, Mabel?" Clarence wondered.

"Well, we have a few more months to go before we need to worry."

"I can always get a job and help out."

"Yes, but it's not necessary. I'll let you know if we get to the desperate place. Meanwhile, I just want to eat."

Clarence had made the salad and put it into the fridge. The potatoes were almost done when he put the steaks on the grill. He sat on a bench and put his feet up and asked, "where do you want to go next, or do you want to stay here for a while? I kind of want to move on and see more of the country. What about Arizona or Wyoming?"

"I've never been to either. I'm game."

CHAPTER FIFTEEN

They had been driving for hours and the scenery all seemed to look alike. There were vast mountain ranges off to the left and sand and more sand to the right. Vegetation was sparse and what there was of it was questionable. Some were cacti and some were plants she had never seen before.

"Look to your right, Mabel." Clarence pointed in the sky at an enormous bird hovering over some carcass. "I think that's a bald eagle getting ready to eat. I wonder what that is on the ground."

"With our luck it will be a dead body and I am not stopping to look. It could be the Governor's wife for all I care. I am not getting involved."

"Aw Mabel. It could be a famous movie star waiting for us to help her."

"It could be the Queen of England for all I care. We don't have the kind of luck that would turn shit to gold. We seem to have a serious lack of good luck, lately. Thank you, but we'll just keep driving without even a close-up look. Another half an hour and it'll be your turn to drive. I want to stop for a while and stretch my legs and maybe get a bite to eat."

"Food sounds good."

For you, food always sounds good."

"I think I'm still growing." They both were laughing when a coyote ran in front of the van. She stood on the braked and the van started to slide but she steered into the slide and the whole thing straightened and she stopped.

"Good Lord, where did that come from? I didn't even see it approach. Did you?" He was shaking his head. They both got out of the van and the coyote was nowhere in sight. "Where did it go?" She asked amazed at the speed of the animal. Buster barked as if to agree with them and went to the nearest rock to leave his mark. He walked around the rock and started growling. Both Mabel and Clarence walked towards Buster to see if he had cornered the coyote but all poor Buster had cornered was a giant tortoise. No head showed and Buster didn't know what to do with it so he started pawing it but the tortoise didn't move.

"Buster!" Clarence chided. "Leave the poor thing

alone." Buster walked back around the rock and sat at his feet.

They finally drove into a small town and got themselves fed. Mabel had chicken and Clarence ate beef. Buster got some leftovers and all were fat and happy as they drove into the campsite.

"We could stay here for a few days. I love the look of this lake and it's quiet here. I need to drown some worms and do some thinking. Why don't you take a nap and I'll cook dinner tonight after I catch my quota. Buster can go with me down by the water."

"That sounds great. I'll do that."

Clarence gathered his fishing gear and a camp seat and trotted off towards the water. Mabel watched until he was out of sight. She unhooked the car from the camper and threw a canvas bag into the front seat. She then went into the van and came out in coveralls and a black haired wig. She had changed into large brown work boots and had gloves in her pockets. She checked the .38 and made sure it was fully loaded and then stuck it into the folds of the coveralls. She knew she had at least three hours before the came back with fish.

She quietly drove off and parked around the corner from the bank and put on a black "Pancho Villa" mustache. She saw that the sidewalk was empty and hurried into the bank and walked up to the teller and handed her a note that said, "Push the button and you die. Cash in brown bag. No dye packs." Very few people noticed her as she was handed a brown bag filled with bills. She nodded at the teller and rushed out of the place. She walked a block and had stripped off the shoes, mustache, wig and coveralls. The gun went into the bottom of a cloth bag. She placed the brown bag into the cloth flight bag and slowly window shopped her way back to the car. She was shaking all over as though she had been in a snow storm. She couldn't get warm and the sun was beating down on her head. She had done it and gotten away with it. "Good God," she would be locked up for the rest of her life foe this. Maybe, Buddy was right and she was getting senile. She had done the unspeakable and wondered how much she had taken from them. She finally quit shaking and started the car when a policeman knocked on her window. She rolled the window down and smiled at him.

"Afternoon, ma'am," he greeted, "have you seen anyone running past your car in the last ten minutes or so?"

"Well to tell the truth. I just got back to the car myself. I was shopping and lost track of the time.

What did this guy look like?" She inquired.

"Approximately six feet or so with black to hair and a mustache," the officer said.

"No, sorry, I haven't seen anyone like that today." She smiled sweetly at him.

He threw a half-hearted salute and thanked her and strolled off to find more people to question. She got the giggles as she watched him saunter away from her car. The tears were rolling down her face by the time she got the car started and she needed to blow her nose to clear her sinuses. She fumbled around her purse and finally came up with an old one. She blew her nose noisily and pulled away from the curb. Another car pulled in front of her and she hit it with a resounding crash.

Damn! Damn and double damn!" she cursed as she watched the policeman turn back to see what happened. She got out of the car and saw that her front left fender was crumpled into the tire and she would not be able to move the car. The other driver was a man around eighty with whisps of white hair around his ears.

"I am so sorry, young lady," he said to her, "I didn't even see you."

"Mr. Ficcarrelli," said the cop, "you did it again. What is this the third or fourth time in the last three months?"

"Yes, I know I should surrender my license but I have no one that can do my driving for me and I was just going to the drugstore to get my prescription filled. I am so sorry."

Mabel was nodding at him and felt sorry for the old guy. He certainly seemed harmless enough when not behind the wheel of the car.

The officer reached into the car and turned it off and handed Mabel the keys.

"Do you have a crowbar in the trunk?" He asked.

Meanwhile, Mr.Ficcarrelli pulled out his insurance card and handed it to Mabel. "Call them and tell them what happened. They'll take care of the car for you. I pay them enough."

She opened the trunk and pulled out the crowbar and handed it to the officer. He took it and placed it into the worst of the dent and started pulling the fender away from the tire. He grunted a few times but finally the fender moved. "I think you can at least drive it home now." She thanked him and returned to the car and pulled away.

When she returned to the campsite, Clarence had the Bar B Que going and six medium sized bass were starting to smell real good.

"Where have you been? I thought that you were sleeping and tried to be quiet. Then, when I went to wake you, you weren't there. Buster couldn't even find you."

"I went to hold up a bank."

"Damn it Mabel, I'm serious. I was worried."

"I went to hold up a bank."

"You're not funny, you know."

"OKAY, I'll tell you. I went to hold up a bank. Come inside a minute."

Clarence left his fish on the grill and went into the camper. Mabel came in a few minutes later carrying a flight bag. She unzipped it and dumped the contents on Clarence's lap.

"There! I told you I held up a bank. Count it!"

She sat across the room and grinned at him. He sat there slack-jawed with money on top of his shoes, lap, and some had fallen clear across the room and the dog was dancing on it.

"Are you serious? Did you really do something that stupid?"

"What do you mean stupid? It was a well-thought out plan and it worked. So, what is your problem?"

"You could have been killed. Something could have gone wrong. Anything."

"Clarence you're a worry wart. I planned it and executed it. I spent months refining it and it took about 1 and a half minutes to do it."

"Maybe Sonny is right. Maybe you are getting senile. My god! How could you put yourself at such risk?"

"What risk? This is a small town. There is no security. There are some tourists and I looked like a man. They are looking for a 6 foot tall guy with black hair and mustache. What risk?"

She bent over and started to pick up the money when he said, "I don't want to lose you. I care too much about you to let you do something like this."

"LET ME?!! Am I a child that I need your permission to do things?"

"I have told you before that if we need money, I can go to work."

"Fine! You go to work and I'll pick you up on the way back."

"Back from where?"

"Back from wherever I decide to take off to without you."

"You would do that?"

"I told you that if you decide to work, we would have to stay in one place and if I had wanted to do that, I would have kept my house and stayed put. I want to see things with or without you."

"So that's the way it is…is that all I mean to you?"

"This is not all about you. This is about me."

"There is a real selfish part of you, woman. I worry about you getting killed and you worry about moving around with or without me."

"Look, Clarence, we made a deal when I sold the house that we were going to travel. I want to see things before I die. Yes, we all die, that is not a part of my worrying. I have been responsible all my life and I want to see things now. I want to breathe mountain air. I want to swim in the ocean. I want to sit in the desert and get a sun burn. I want to swim in a waterfall. I want to walk through huge luscious forests and I can't do any of those things if I sit in one place. I raised my kid and husband and then it was a series of jobs and friendships and I have always been the one to be responsible. I want to let my hair down and soar. Do you understand?" She had tears in her eyes as she finished her tirade.

He came to her and placed her in his protective embrace. "Yeah, I think I do. Although you need to understand that I'm a natural worrier and forgive me if I worry about you." "I know. Let's go for a walk."

CHAPTER SIXTEEN

She had this bank thing pretty much down pat now. The first robbery had netted her a cool eight thousand and the second one was almost thirteen thousand. She had changed her disguises and never once was suspected of being the robber. Clarence kept trying to talk her out of this dangerous behavior but she kept reassuring him that there was nothing to worry about.

At three in the morning she heard a scream and awoke to find that it came from her. She sat up in bed and realized that she was soaking wet with sweat from the nightmare. Clarence knocked on the door and she told him to come in. He sat at the side of the bed and asked if she wanted to talk about whatever was bothering her and she nodded. She began, "When I was twelve, my little brother was staying with our grandpa for a month. It was kind of a vacation for him. Grandpa would take him fishing

EXTRACTION

in his row boat and the two would have, 'guy days.' There would be no girls allowed. I thought that this was great for my little brother. So, it was the last day and I rode my bike over to grandpa's house and the door was open. So, I walked in and heard some mumbling from the bedroom. I opened the door and thought that grandpa and Mike were wrestling. Then I saw that grandpa was lying on Mike's back whispering, 'my sweet boy' and Mike was moaning, 'please don't, please don't.' I saw that Mike's butt was exposed and grandpa covered his legs. And Mike's moans were like a little animal in pain. That's when I realized that grandpa had his thing in Mike's rear and it must have hurt Mike. I saw red. I grabbed what little hair grandpa had on his head and pulled and pulled until he was screaming. Grandpa turned his head and bit me in the wrist and I still wouldn't let go. Mike was fully dressed by then and I still held on to the old man's hair. Mike nudged me and said, 'I'm not gonna get my go cart now because I didn't finish grandpa's game.' I let go of his hair and looked at Mike in astonishment. He was only seven so this was hard to explain to him. I told him that what grandpa was doing was BAD and he shouldn't be doing that to little boys. The old man finally let go of my wrist and as Mike and I were leaving, he threatened both of us.

Mike was angry with me about the go cart and I was furious with grandpa. I put Mike on the handle bars and rode home. When I told MA what happened, she went ballistic and started pounding on me calling me a liar and then she screamed that her father would never do anything like that and I better never say anything like that again. She emphasized each line with a knock to my head and shoulders and back. She viscously turned to Mike and asked him what happened and he said, 'Nothing.' There I was with his set of tooth marks in my forearm and bruises all over my body and had no backup on what happened. My life at home was 'hell' after that and grandpa went on as before and Mike spent many a night there. Grandpa would be at my house for Christmas and Thanksgiving like I never saw anything. I would duck him every chance I got. Of course, Ma was furious with me because I didn't 'act' right for her. Mike hung and killed himself when he was thirteen and Ma started drinking. One night, she was pretty loaded, she admitted that grandpa had tried to have sex with her too. I could no longer feel anything for her and when I was seventeen, I left her house and never went back."

"Oh, God, Mabel. I wish that I could have been there for you. I would have understood."

"You're sweet but weren't even born yet." She patted his cheek. "I need a shower and need to change the linens on my bed. We both need to sleep."

She grabbed a clean nightgown and went into the bathroom to shower. When she came out, Clarence had changed her bed already. She thanked him and crawled under the covers and was sound asleep in seconds.

In gratitude, she made him a huge breakfast of pancakes, bacon and eggs. He sat down and started eating like it was his last meal. He was on his fourth pancake when he finally looked up from his plate and said, "Man, these are great. You could open a restaurant with this recipe. I never ate pancakes this good before. Is this an old family recipe?"

She grinned and said, "Buddy, when he was little, would try to guess what I had added to his pancakes. Sometimes it was cinnamon, sometimes a little vanilla and sometimes fruit. We used to have fun with this but of course, he outgrew that."

She continued to cook and he continued to eat in compatible silence.

When he finished, he wiped his mouth and

burped loudly and said, "Where next?"

"I really want to see the state of Washington and perhaps Oregon. I hear the fishing is great there and want to explore all the little islands there."

"Do we leave today or tomorrow?" he asked as he fed Buster the last pancake."

"Stop feeding him from the table. It's not good for him and then he will be a pain every time we eat anything."

"OK. OK no big deal."

"Let's leave in the morning. I don't feel very rested today. We can get an early start."

"I think that Buster and I are going to fish for a while. Want to come?"

"No. You go ahead. I'm ready to clean up around here and get ready for the traveling tomorrow. I'll lock stuff down."

CHAPTER SEVENTEEN

She was awed by the size of the fir trees in Tacoma. You couldn't see the sky because they were so high that they met at the top and blocked out the light. Mile after mile of huge trees and beautiful scenery. Small lakes peeked through the foliage and everywhere were campers and trailers. She loved this place. Just inside of Tacoma, they saw the Space Needle looming toward the sky. From afar, it looked like it would be some type of kiddieland ride but in actuality it held a restaurant on top.

"I want to eat there," she announced. "It would be like eating on top of the world."

"How about we look for a campsite first and then dress up and stroll around."

"Fine."

They drove toward Seattle and saw a sign for KOA and pulled into a rural road. The offices were on the left and she went into the small shack to register them. They wanted her license plate number, home address and a nearest relative. His name plate said, "Al."

"Wow. This is the first place that asked for all of this," she commented to the ranger.

"We've had a few problems here. It's for your protection, really." The short man in the green uniform replied.

"What kind of problems?" she wanted to know.

"We had a murder and a few break ins."

"Here? In this campground?"

"Yes, normally we don't have a high crime rate but last month put us on the map." She realized that he was a gossip and she might as well find out all she could.

"So, who got killed?"

"The wife of a camper. They had been here a few days and she suddenly disappeared after having gone swimming. He looked all over the place for her and finally called us. We got the dogs looking and one found the body under a thick brush. She had been partially buried in about two feet of dirt. The coroner said that she was strangled and raped. In that order. She was a pretty blonde who had only been married a year. Thank God they had no kids. We're trying to figure out if the break ins are related or a separate crime."

"How awful for that poor husband. He must be devastated. To go on a vacation and come home with no wife."

"Yeah! It's awful. You be careful OK?"

"I have a body-guard," she reassured him. "He'll keep me safe."

He gave her a campsite number and pointed to the other side of the lake. "That's where you're at. Be safe."

She smiled and thanked him and went back to the camper.

"Geez, what took you so long?"

"A murder."

"What?"

"They had a murder here."

"What?"

"A young lady was found buried here. The husband is still camping here waiting for word of the murder."

"We don't want to stay here, do we? I don't feel we need the flack."

"I want to stay. This place is perfect," said Mabel smiling.

"I know that look. What are you up to now?" Clarence questioned.

"Oh, nothing."

"Bull. I know you. You've got something up your sleeve and it's not a good thing, by your look. It is probably something horrible."

"Clarence, you worry too much. Take a chill pill."

"Look, lady. I know what an evil plotting mind you have and your look says that you are getting ready to pull something."

"Enough. I'm going for a nice long walk, come on Buster let's walk."

"Be careful. He's not much of protection."

CHAPTER EIGHTEEN

They walked and walked, enjoying the fresh air and the scenery. They stopped and watched a few kids throwing a Frisbee around. Buster, being Buster, ran and caught one thrown by the younger boy who laughed uproariously and petted Buster like he had done something wonderful. Buster relished in the attention from the kids and his tail wagged furiously.

"Come on, let's walk some more. Bye, kids." She waved and kept walking. Buster was panting to catch up with her.

She was surprised to find herself near the guard-shack and Al waved at her as she was about to pass it. "Hey," he greeted. "How are things at your campsite? All quiet, I hope."

"Yes, we love it here. It is so restful and picturesque. This is really the most beautiful part of the country that we've seen."

"I was born and raised here and don't know much about the rest of the country but I tell you, I love fishing with all my heart. No meal is better than fresh caught fish."

She nodded in agreement and said, "What about the murder, is there any news?"

He shook his head and said, "No, as a matter of fact there was another one on the other side of the lake. They found her pretty much the same way as the other one. Partially dressed and under a thick bush. She had also been raped and worst of all they found bite marks again. Whoever it was just about chewed her breast off." He remarked in disgust.

She looked pensive and said, "I'll think about this and get back to you. This kind of reminds me of a murderer we had at the jail I was working at and he used to brag about the killings like he was God and could determine who lived or died. He was proud of what he had done. The other inmates left him alone because they thought that he had a screw loose."

"Didn't he?" Al asked.

"No, he was a sociopath. He believed that what he was doing was O.K. and that laws did not apply to him. He was charming and polite but would kill you, cut you up and eat lunch over your body without batting an eye. He was really likeable and had an artistic flair. He drew roses with tear drops and left them on a nurse's desk, daily. He was so good with words that he conned the jail nurse into helping him escape. She was young and gullible and her body was found two days after he escaped. He had cut her to ribbons, stole her car and cleaned out her bank account. He was found not far from her apartment. When captured, he said that she deserved to die because she had helped him escape."

"Good Lord. What an animal. What happened to him?"

"He was executed."

"Good! Do you suppose our killer is a sociopath, too?"

"I don't know but he sure is killing them fast. Was the second on blond too?"

"Yes, they could have been sisters. She was here with her parents. They were on a celebration trip because she had just graduated college and wanted to spend some time together. A very nice family. I wish I could find this bastard."

"See you later, Al. If you feel like it, drop by for a drink later by the campfire."

He nodded and waved as she walked away with Buster at her heels. "You are such a gook dog." She bent down and patted him. "Let's head back and take the car to town and pick up a couple of steaks and a few salad making ingredients. I also have a taste for some hard rolls slathered with butter. Hungry? Let's go and you can have dinner too."

CHAPTER NINETEEN

They found the third body the next morning right near the water. She was also blond and had on no clothes. Visible bite marks covered her torso and the police had roped off the entire area. Clarence was angry because he had no access to the water. Mabel decided that with all the cops here, there would be very few in town and it would be a good time to strike. She almost ran to the car to get to the bank.

As before, there were no hitches. She walked in, produced the note and walked out with a bag of money. NOTHING TO IT! No police and no security. She liked these little towns that did not bother with security in the bank because no one would hold them up.

She drove back to the campsite after ditching her clothes again in a dumpster two blocks from the bank and activity was still strong near the water.

Cops were everywhere. They must have borrowed some from other towns because she counted at least twenty. Some were on their hands and knees and some were sifting sand through a strainer looking for clues.

Their campsite was so close to the murder that she could overhear some of the conversation, "This bastard is different from the others. The bites don't match. "See here," the coroner pointed to the left breast, "this canine tooth is different fro the other that I examined. Dammit! We might have three separate killers here which means the Feds will be here soon and we will have nothing to say about anything. We have got to find him soon." He was obviously talking to the police chief who was nodding vigorously and agreeing.

"Are you sure about the bite marks?"

"What do you mean am I sure?"

"Your lab guys couldn't have made a mistake and it is the same guy?"

"I took impressions and they don't match. No way. All three are different as day and night. This is three different guys. Or a copycat."

"Jesus, we have loonies running around in a secluded campsite killing blonds. No trace, no clues, no hint of who this monster is. I'm so frustrated that I could drink all night and kick the shit out of anybody looking at me cross-eyed."

"Maybe we'll get a break soon. No one is that good that they can keep this up without getting caught."

Mabel overheard all this and was thinking about it when Al approached and sat near her.

"Want a cold drink, Al?" she asked.

"Don't mind if I do."

She brought him a soft drink and sat companionable next to him. They were silent for a while when he said, "You know the bank got held up but all the excitement around here that ain't nothing compared to the murders. Chief ain't even gonna look for the perp. Has his hands full with these killers. Man, I wish that I could nail this bastard. That would take me out of this shit-hole and back in the street."

"You were a cop?"

"Yeah, once upon a time. I was answering a call from a battered woman and a little kid ran out in front of the squad car."

"Did he die?"

"NO, worse. He's crippled for life and I was found guilty of negligence. Rangers took me because out here I can only hit a coyote or a bear." He grinned sardonically.

"Good lord. How sad. Is the little boy O.K. now?"

"No, he'll never be O.K. but he is walking with aid of canes but his life won't be the same because of me."

She grabbed his forearm and looked deep into his eyes and said, "Al, it was an accident.

Both of you don't have to suffer."

"You don't understand." He shook his head from side to side. "His mother was a woman that I was seeing on the side. She thinks that I hit her kid deliberately. She pressed the charges. Her husband didn't know we were seeing each other until my hearing. That little boy just ran out between two parked cars and there I was. I had nightmares for months. I kept seeing the kid over and over flying over the hood of the squad car. I can still hear the sound of the impact. It will haunt me forever. I should have been going slower."

"How long ago did this happen?"

"Almost nine years." His long thin face began to pucker as though he was going to cry.

"So for nine years you have been beating yourself up over an accident?"

He nodded.

"Al, people fall down stairs, they get hit by trains and buses, they get murdered, lighting hits them and other things un-expectantly happen. It is not your fault. Anyone could have driven down that street and hit him. Why wasn't he in the house? Where was his mother? Al, you need to let this go and move on."

"I went to therapy for a while and they said the same thing. I need to look forward, not backward. All my worrying and fretting isn't going to make the kid O.K."

"You need to focus on positive things. Find the killer."

Al roared. A belly laugh so loud and long that the cops sifting the sand stopped sifting and looked at him. The laughter died down and he actually giggled at Mabel.

"Me find a killer. That's rich. Me. I got kicked off the force. Me. Find the killer."

"You're not stupid. Logic and reasoning can find him. There aren't three killers. There's one and one only. He's clever and trying to make it look like there are copycats. There aren't any more killers. Look at the odds. Small town with no history of violence in twenty years. In a period of a month, you have three murders. Three! Does not compute."

"I think I see what you're saying but how can that be?"

"I have a few ideas but you would have to check a few things for me?"

"Like what?"

"The first woman that got killed, is there a history of violence in the family? Has he ever hit her? Was their marriage working?"

"You think he did her in and then killed the rest to cover up? Good lord, he'd have to be an animal to do that."

"Most killers kill to make room for someone new in their lives. Like maybe a girlfriend or a co-worker that he's involved with. Why after a year of marriage did they come so far from home? Didn't someone say that they were from New Jersey?"

"Yes, up East somewhere."

"How convenient to go on a camping trip and have your wife die."

"You really think he did it?"

"Has he been checked out?"

"I expect the state boys would have done that, wouldn't you?"

"Or they're feeling sorry for him, after all the poor guy is a widower now."

"Man, if I could only prove it."

"We'll see. Another drink?"

"No, I've got to get back to work. The captain also

is using us to try to find the bank robber and we're supposed to check people who suddenly have money. This is a joke."

"Sounds like it. Do you ask people after they spend money whether of not they held up the bank?"

"It is dumb but they don't have a clue. We're just fishing. The one thing we do know is that the guy isn't black. That's about it."

"See you Al." He got up and threw a salute at her and jumped into his golf cart and puttered away.

CHAPTER TWENTY

"Look, Clarence, $13,768.42. This is the most I've gotten. And no one has a clue because of the murders. For a little bank, they sure had a lot of cash on hand. Must be the payroll for the entire town." She felt like a young girl who had won a prize.

Clarence did not look happy. He worried about the risks she was taking and she did not seem to care that he was worried. He did not know how to get through to her and have her understand his feelings. She appeared to be "high" after each time she did it and it would take days for her to come off the "high." He was concerned that she was getting addicted to the rush of getting away with the robberies. He looked at her smiling at the stack of money sorted neatly on the coffee table. She had a pile of twenties stacked neatly to the stack of tens and then fives. The singles made four stacks on their own. She appeared happy. That's the look he was trying to put on her face and could not succeed to do. He found that he was jealous of her new hobby. This seemed to satisfy something in her that he could not. DAMN!

"This was the easiest yet," she noted. "They didn't even have a 90 yr. watchman. I bet I could hit them again."

"Mabel, I'm not going to preach to you but this is a very dangerous game you're playing. Not every place you hit is going to be easy and sooner or later you'll be caught or shot."

"Sweetheart, you worry too much for a young man. All my life I have played by society's rules. I'm having fun now. If I die, oh, well. That's how we met. You threatened to kill me."

"I never threatened you. I have learned to care about you these last few months and I would be devasted if something happened to you. I just want you to know how much you mean to me."

"I know, but I won't stop. But, I'll promise to be careful." She patted him on the shoulder. "I think you need to see a woman. You're getting that antsy feel about you again."

"Like last time?" he laughed. "That worked out fine."

"Not all women are like that little gold-digger. She

was not for you. You need to find a sweetie-pie."

"Clarence, you're being a jerk."

"I'm just joking around. I think it was a lot safer when we were hitting Maury up for money. This bank thing really has me worried."

"Maybe we should consider him for another one. It's been a while."

"I'll go online and see what I can do. I need to contribute to this family anyway."

"I wonder how Marie is doing. I miss her. Maybe, I'll give her a call and see."

"Hello, may I speak to Marie please? What? WHAT DID YOU SAY?" she screamed into the phone. "Oh my God! When did it happen? She was doing so well. O.K. Bye."

She hung up and started crying long heavy sobs. Clarence simply put his arms around her and led her to the couch. He placed her head on his chest and held her tight. She was gasping for air and crying like a little kid. He handed her a tissue and she loudly blew her nose and continued to cry.

Time passed and Clarence asked gently, "Did she pass?"

"That bastard killed her with his antics!" She announced between hiccups. "She loved him and he treated her like shit. Always another woman, always another piece. She was never enough for him. She died and he gets all the insurance money from her death. The little weasel. He should be the one gone. The world would be better off without him. She was a wonderful person. He is an ugly little toad that needs to be squashed. I could kill him myself."

Clarence let her ventilate and kept patting her shoulder trying to soothe the obvious pain that she was feeling. But, she would not be soothed. "I want to dry him out. I want him to be as broke as he was when he married her. She had the career and the house. He had nothing, not even a job. She got that for him too through her connections. Everything he did and accomplished was her doing it for him. Instead of being happy with her, her had to hurt her. Their entire marriage was based on lies. Where was he when she had to have surgery? Do you know that he 'hit' on her nurse? She was in bed recuperating from her first breast operation and this little piece of shit was trying to touch the nurse. Thank God the nurse had more sense and slapped his face. I saw this with my own eyes. Marie was drugged up with morphine and slept through the whole thing. I lost all or what little respect I had for the man right then and there. I started to make excuses with Marie to not visit when the weasel was home and only take Marie out for lunch when he was not around."

Her crying had subsided and now the anger was coming through loud and clear. Clarence preferred her angry over sad. Anger, he could handle. Her crying made him want to cry too and that was not cool. He was having extremely deep feelings for this funny lady who was as unpredictable as a six year old with a temper tantrum. He really loved/respected her strength and kindness. Her every day level demeanor. She rarely had fits of rage or mood swings. She was fun to have around and like a good laugh. She was a "good" woman with a big heart and often went out of her way to help others but she could not tolerate "B.S." and let people know that she couldn't. Her obsession with money worried him. They were living a simple life with very few needs. Gas, food, dog food, and a few minor pleasures. She loved her chocolate. All except the dark kind. He sometimes came from town with a Swedish chocolate bar for her and she would act like a little kid and savor it and smack her lips. He had a weakness for ice cream. The two were so matched. Why couldn't she see that. They were good for each other and to each other. A few years

EXTRACTION

between them held her from going further. He could not get her to see reason.

"I want to see her grave and then I want to fleece that bastard until he has nothing left. What a human piece of shit he is." Mabel spoke through clenched teeth. She went outside the camper and, of course Buster followed her. He sat on her foot, which was something new so that she could not escape him and put his head on her knee. Her hands were folded in a prayerful way and Buster lifted them until they fell on his head and she absently started stroking him. He was in "doggie bliss."

Clarence came out and sat next to her and reached for her hand. She let him hold it and it was comforting to her without any feeling of romance. Clarence looked at it as "progress." She loved Buster unconditionally but liked Clarence like a younger brother. As she was contemplating how to take what Maury had, Al drove up and screeched to a halt maybe a foot from her chair.

"Jesus Mabel, we got another one. She was found inside a row boat floating on the lake. Her breast was almost bitten off. This guy is escalating and the sheriff still thinks that each murder is done by a different killer. What an idiot. This has to be one guy. I thought about what you said but the only problem is that each set of teeth if different according to forensics. This last one had an overbite almost like buck teeth. The last one had a tooth missing in the front. Now the Core of Army Engineers people are talking about closing the campground down. I'll be out of a job and maybe have to give the bank robber competition. Damn, I can't afford to lose my job." He looked depressed and sighed so hard that Buster went to him and placed his chin on Al's leg. Al absentmindedly stroked the dog.

"Where is that husband of the first woman, now?" Mabel asked.

"He's still here on the grounds. The State Police restricted him to the campsite until further notice, Why?"

"Does this guy have a job? What is his background? Criminal history? Girlfriend? What is the deal with him? How come none of his family is here with him? Or hers for that matter? Why is he alone?"

"Well, according to records, he has no priors; works for a computer company in R&D, but is friendly with one of the secretaries. No one is willing to say whether or not they are more than friends or they don't know. She has no family and he is estranged from his since his teens. He claims parental abuse in his childhood. Her parents died in a plane crash a few years ago and a sharp lawyer sued the airline and she came into quite a bit of dough from that. GOD! What great motive to OFF someone. The almighty love of money. I bet he did it. I'm just not smart enough to figure out how. I would love to nail him. He is so smug under his phony grieving for his dear departed wife."

"Al, find out the last time he went to a dentist and what he had done."

Al looked at her as if she had lost her mind, "Do what?"

"Find out when he went to a dentist and for what. I think this guy has false teeth and probably has a few set of them. Dentists are now making temporary denture that fit over real teeth to change the smile of a person and maybe our guy has those. Check out Easr first. Dentists have records."

"Wow! Mabel you may be on to something here. My God, then if he killed her and killed the others, he is really getting a taste for murder."

"No he didn't just get a taste. He's been doing this for a while; he's too sophisticated to be a new killer and he cleans his trail real well to be impulsive. This is a hardnosed, cold-blooded murderer who enjoys what he does. He's hoping all you Rubes are too stupid to catch him."

Al nodded and nodded in agreement. "I'm gonna do some checking and get back to you. I'll start with his dentist on the East Coast." He jumped up and almost tripped over Buster who caught Al's enthusiasm and jumped up as Al was stepping over him.

Clarence looked at her and sighed, "He knows about you and the bank."

"How could he know?"

"I don't have a clue but he does. You didn't catch his innuendo about joining the bank robber."

"He was just kidding. He doesn't know anything."

"He's not stupid as he looks, Mabel."

"Relax. I still have Maury on my mind. I want everything he has and then some. Think of something."

"If we get Maury, will you give up the banks?"

"Maybe. If the haul is big enough."

"What's big enough? 50,000, 100,000, or half a million?"

"Half a million sounds about enough to retire on." She smiled at him. "Any ideas?"

"Let me think on it."

EXTRACTION

"Let's run Buster down by the lake and see what the cops found and maybe Al will catch up with us. Meanwhile keep thinking."

She walked and Clarence and the dog ran ahead.

CHAPTER TWENTY-ONE

They went to bed around eleven after taking a long walk and eating a light meal. Buster munched happily on the bone of a steak and she tried to sleep but thinking of different ways to get Maurie's money kept her from sleep, "Wake up! Wake up!" Clarence yelled, pulling her arm.

She looked at the clock and said, "It's 2:30 in the morning. Have you lost your mind?"

"No, I just found it. Listen, I have an idea. GOLD."

"Gold?" What about it?"

"We send him a nugget and tell him we have found a gold-mind and this is a small sample. Then we ask for money to finish mining and he gets half of what we find. It's perfect."

She sat up in bed and decided that coffee would bring her all the way around and she could think better. She swung her legs over the side and made her way to the coffee pot. She measured out the

EXTRACTION

three required scoops, added a pinch of salt and water and waited for the smell to take over.

"Tell me again," she slurped her hot coffee, "what about the gold?"

He picked his cup up and explained, "We get some gold things and melt them down into nuggets. We tell Maury that we have found a gold vein in California and we need investment money to finish mining it. He won't have what we ask for and will most likely, 'borrow' from his investors but we tell him that he can have the money returned in a week or so because we have other people going in with us. He will be skeptical but then, we send him the nugget. Of course, he'll take it to an appraiser and the appraiser will tell him that the gold is real. Maury willbecome secretive and smug about what he is going to do. Then we email him a newspaper article on the gold strike and that will send him over to us with both hands filled with money. The bait will be too strong for him to resist. What do you think?" He finally took a breath and smiled at her.

She felt like she had a hangover and one single cup of coffee was not curing it. She knew that it was the lack of sleep but she felt the blood pumping through her with excitement of this idea. She decided that a shower would clear her head and they could talk some more afterwards. She felt the hot water run over her and smiled. The idea was crazy enough to work. Maury was greedy and they had the bait.

She came out of the bathroom dressed in shorts and a pink T-shirt. She asked Clarence if he wanted to go to breakfast in town and he also got dressed in shorts and a tank top. The prediction for the weather was heat and more heat.

Clarence drove into the small town and found its only restaurant, coffee shop and parked in front of the door. A smiling woman of forty or so greeted them warmly and asked if they wanted coffee. They both nodded and read the menu.

"I'll have the waffles with fresh strawberries." Mabel announced.

"Gee, that sounds great but I'll have the peaches instead." Clarence delared.

"We need to kill some time until the pawn shops open." Clarence said. "It's only six thirty. I want to see how much it will cost us to make a decent nugget."

"I imagine it will be about three or four hundred at the most. Do we have enough?"

"Clarence, we're fine. Don't worry."

The waitress came with two plates covered with

EXTRACTION

whipped cream and fruit peeking out from underneath the white mound. She place the plates in front of them and said, "Enjoy! Anything else? More coffee?" Both nodded and she poured the steaming liquid into their cups. She left them and walked back towards the cook, who was leaning on the half-wall smiling at her.

"Give me your cell phone." Clarence reached for it and started hitting button.

"Hey, man. It's me Clarence. How you been? The kids? The old lady? Cool. Hey, look, I need a favor you. Yeah, I'll pay. I need to know how much a guy is worth and how much an insurance policy paid. How long will it take? Last name is Edelstein, first name Maury or Maurice. Deceased wife's name was Marie. I'll call back in four hours or so. Will that be enough time? O.K. talk to you then." He hit the disconnect button and smiled at Mabel.

"He'll know to the penny how much our boy is worth and then you can figure out how to handle that. O.K. talk to you then." He hit disconnect button and smiled at Mabel.

"He'll know to the penny how much our boy is worth and then you can figure out how to handle that. O.K.?" He grinned and sipped more coffee.

"Who is this mystery man?" Mabel wanted to know.

"Just a guy I know who can hack into anything. He is pretty much legit but will do a little on the side for a buck or two. How's your waffle? Mine is delicious."

"Mine too. Oh, look who's here!"

Al plopped himself into the booth next to Clarence and announced, "Two eggs scrambled, Greek toast, three strips of extra crispy bacon and coffee, Sugar."

He turned to Mabel and said, "We nailed his ass. No, YOU nailed him but I got the credit for great thinking. He confessed to eleven murders and in four different states. You were right all along. Teeth were the answer. He had two sets of dentures and a set of those teeth that go over existing teeth. He changed his bite three different ways. He thought we were hicks and none of us could outsmart him. He has married four of the women and he's not from Philly at all; he from Chicago. He's left a trail of bodies all over the country. Right now, he's singing about where he buried them."

He jumped up and grabbed Mabel and kissed her full on the lips, all the while keeping an eye on Clarence to see how he would react. Clarence just grinned at him.

"And best of all, since I solved it, hee hee, I got my

old job back and a possible promotion I feel like a little kid on Christmas day. No dentist out East heard of our boy and when we questioned his dental work, he started singing. He knew we had him. We got a search warrant for the trailer and THERE they were. All the different sets of teeth. THANK YOU, THANK MABEL and can I ask one favor of you?"

"Sure, Al what is it?"

"Stay the hell out of our bank! O.K."

She laughed and patted his cheek. "Sure. We were thinking of moving on, any way. We have other fish to fry."

"Damn woman. Clarence is one lucky guy to know someone like you. I wish I could go with you guys."

"NO WAY, DUDE! Your ass stays here and keeps the city clean and crime free."

Clarence growled at him.

CHAPTER TWENTY-TWO

She was packing up the kitchen when Clarence walked in, "You know that Al knew didn't you?"

"He only suspects: doesn't know anything."

"I think you're wrong. He's not as dumb as you think he is."

"So what? What if he does know? What is he going to do? I saved his butt and he is thrilled."

"I just think that you're not as sick as you think you are and are in danger of screwing up."

"I know that I sound like a broken record but I worry and if that rat-faced Al can figure it out, just think what the FBI and do to you."

"But the Feds have great prisons with tennis courts and swimming pools." She kidded.

"That's not funny, woman."

"Please, not again. I've heard all this before. Why don't you help me lock down and we can get on our way? California or Wyoming?"

EXTRACTION

"Well, I think California because that dumb Maury will associate gold with California and gold rush."

"You're probably right. California here we come."

Clarence drove through Oregon while Mabel admired the sights. When they hit the border, Clarence pulled over and got out to stretch. He yawned loudly and she laughed and asked him if he wanted her to drive.

He nodded and said, "I'm really beat. I need a nap."

"Shall I tuck you in?"

"Go take your nap. Buster, come back here now." She laughed as he frolicked in the long sage grass and tried to pee on anything taller than him. He bounced and bounced around and looked like he was trying to make up for the long ride. He got halfway toward her when he yelped and fell over.

"Clarence! Clarence, quick!" She yelled. Clarence ran out I his boxer shorts and she just pointed towards Buster. Clarence ran to him and picked him up in one arm and carried him to the trailer. Clarence placed him on the table and started examining him inch by inch.

"Damn!" Clarence declared loudly, "get me a razor blade and that turkey baster and some bandages. Snake bite."

She moved quickly and watched Clarence cut an H into Buster's leg. He used the turkey baster to suck out the venom Buster yelped and Mabel gently stroked his head while Clarence kept using the baster on him. Finally, it seemed that there was nothing but blood in it and he put antiseptic and a dressing on the wound.

"Don't you chew on that Buster. I want to see that in the same place tomorrow. O.K.?"

The dog just looked at him and as Clarence went to pet him, Buster threw his tounge out and licked Clarence on the hand.

"I think that he just thanked you." Laughed Mabel, "Do you think that he needs to go to the vet?"

"No, I think that we got to him quick enough. He'll be fine. We'll keep an eye on him just in case."

By this time Buster was running around like the whole thing never happened. Mabel was assured by the dog's behavior and started to get into the camper when a state trooper pulled up. "Where you folks heading?" He asked with a stern face.

"Well, we're going to San Diego on vacation." She smiled sweetly at the man.

"Who is this dark guy with you?" He frowned, obviously prejudiced. He nodded toward Clarence.

"Oh, do you mean my son, Officer Marlow? Do you have a problem with him being darker than me? Isn't there a course out here in the academy on 'race relation?"

"Let's see you drivers license and registration. PLEASE."

The sarcasm was obvious and Mabel could feel herself getting angry at this red-necks stupidity and ignorance. Clarence was alarmed looking at her and her tight face. He just hoped that she wouldn't do anything too stupid.

"What might be your probable cause for all this?" She asked him, her chin jutting out.

"She handed over her license and registration and asked him if there was anything he wanted?" She was furious.

"I want to see his I.D." He pointed at Clarence.

"NO!" Mabel said.

"What did you say, lady?"

"I said, NO. There are laws against this type of harassment, officer and I will not stand for it. We have done absolutely nothing for you to act this way. My license is clean, my registration is fine and I want you to call a sergeant or other supervisor right now." She crossed her arms.

This was not a good sign, though Clarence. She is in "fighting mode." This woman is seriously mad enough to end up in jail. Damn.

Officer Marlowe asked, "What do you need a supervisor for?"

"Call him." Her arms were still crossed and her chin jutted out defiantly. She uncrossed her arms and speed dialed the 911 number without pulling the cell phone out of her pocket.

"What are you doing?" the Trooper asked her.

She smiled as another squad car pulled up and a LT. stepped out and placed his hat on his head. "Hi there." She greeted the newcomer.

"What's going on here?" He asked his trooper and before Marlowe could open his mouth, Mabel explained how they were stopped for no probable cause and the racial remark.

"Go back to the barracks, Marlowe! That's an order! I don't want to hear anything form you."

Marlowe spun around and quickly walked back to his squad but before he sat, he shot her a look of naked hatred. Mabel smiled at him sweetly and turned back to the Lt.

"I am so sorry folks. We have had a few problems with him. He is already on probation and I really don't want you to think that Californians are unhospitable. Let me say it, WELCOME TO CALIFORNIA. I am sorry again for the hassle and I hope you enjoy your stay with us." He reached out his hand to Clarence and they shook Mabel thanked him for relieving them and they got into the camper and slowly pulled away.

"I'm worried about that Marlowe guy." Clarence confided.

"Don't worry about him. I can take care of myself. Let's find a campsite and get some rest. I think both of us are tired. You park and I'll get groceries and we'll have a nice meal by a campfire. The hell with worrying about Marlowe."

Shortly they came upon the site assigned to them and Clarence unhooked the car while Mabel got her purse and started to make a list of supplies they would need. Milk, eggs, bread, butter and orange juice. A couple of steaks, a few potatoes, and fixing for a salad. She checked the fridge and they had enough salad dressing. What she really wanted was some garlic bread. She wrote it down and told Clarence that she'd be back in an hour and for him to have the fire going. He nodded and told her to be careful driving.

She pulled out of the campsite and drove the required 20 miles per hour until she got to the first cross street. She did the speed limit and was surprised to see the red flashing lights behind her. "He must be going to an emergency." She thought but he did not pass her.

CHAPTER TWENTY-THREE

Clarence sat by the fire and looked at his watch. She had told an hour and that was three hours ago. His stomach was rumbling and he thought about the last time he panicked and it turned out to be nothing. He grabbed a couple of pieces of cheese and stuffed them in hid mouth. Something was better than nothing. Maybe she had a flat and if he came to her rescue, she would be angry with him. Damn that stubborn mule of a woman. Where was she???

He and the dog paced around the fire that was dying out. While Clarence worried, the dog marked out his territory. His cell phone rang and he did not recognize the number. He answered and was told that Mabel had had an accident and he needed to come to the hospital.

"Damn it! That woman was going to turn his hair gray." He got a ride with a fellow camper and was let out at the emergency room entrance. He asked for the female accident victim and the nurse, without looking up from her paper work, pointed to room two. He promptly marched to the room and saw a doctor working on someone he did not recognize and was going to excuse himself from the room when her hand reached up to hold his hand.

His stomach flipped and the tears came streaming down his face when he realized it was Mabel. She looked as though she was wearing a disguise. Her nose was three times its size and both eyes were swollen shut. Her lips were bloody and swollen and the doctor was tying off the last sutures in her scalp. The doctor told her that he would be back in a minute and left the room.

Clarence came closer to her, still holding her hand which he saw also bloody and swollen.

"Clarence, follow my lead," she mumbled.

"What happened? Did you hit someone with the car? Are you hurt anywhere else?"

She slowly shook her head. "Oh God, it really hurts." Tears escaped her swollen eyelids.

Clarence walked over to the Kleenex and gently wiped her tears, not wanting to do further damage.

"No accident." She mumbled.

The doctor returned with x-ray films and while

putting a dressing over the sutures told her that they would dissolve in a few days but that she had to keep them dry. He told her that her ribs were not broken but badly bruised and she needed to get plenty of rest.

"You are a very lucky lady that you didn't get killed when that truck hit you." He stated.

She nodded and looked at Clarence and he winked in comprehension. She is not telling the doctor the truth. The poor thing. She looks like she went nine rounds with Tyson.

"Well Liz," said the doctor, "you can go home but look out for symptoms like dizziness or vomiting. If that happens, you need to come back ASAP."

"Thank you, doctor." She mumbled.

Clarence helped her get dressed and lifted her off the examining table. He held her so tight that she let out a small cry of pain.

"Where is the car?" He asked.

She pointed to the far end of the lot. He led her to a bench and helped her sit. "I'll be right back. Don't move." He sprinted across the lot.

Shortly he pulled up and jumped from the vehicle and gently helped her into the car and buckled her seat belt.

"Do you wan to tell me?" He probed.

"Not now, later." She rested her head against his arm and started to snore.

He put her to bed and filled a baggie with ice and placed it over her swollen eyes.

"Sleep for a while and when you wake, I'll make you some soup."

She nodded and tried to smile but her lips felt frozen and barely moved.

She slept for two hours and when he heard her stirring, he brought her the soup. He sat at the side of the bed and spoon-fed her. He wondered what had happened. She was simply going for groceries and ended up looking like a battered wife. He would wait and see what she told him. He felt irritable and anxious but did not know why. Maybe it was because he was supposed to protect her and had no clue as to how she got hurt.

She woke up moaning and he saw that her lip was bleeding but the ice had brought the swelling down. There was blood all over the pillow case and somehow that really enraged him. HIS MABEL WAS BLEEDING.

Surprisingly she finished all the soup and thanked him for it. He offered her a pain pill but she refused.

"What happened?" He asked gently as he took her

into his arms, more for comfort and his own needs than anything else.

She turned her head and started crying.

"Tell me."

"Was driving to the store, speeding a little, got pulled over, flashing light. Cop opened my door, hit me in the face. I bled and he pulled me out of the car. Beat and beat me. I fall on the ground and he left."

"I AM GOING TO KILL THAT SONOFABITCH! I am going to kill his dumb ass."

Clarence raged.

"No! We go to Vegas." She said.

"No! I WANT HIM! That weaseling bastard has to hit on a woman. I'll get him."

"NO! He'll shoot you."

"Mabel relax. You need more sleep so you feel better. I'll get more ice." He helped her lay back on the clean pillow and changed the bloody pillow case for a nice clean one. He returned with a fresh bag of ice and placed it on her mouth.

"Still hungry?" He asked.

She shook her head and nodded off.

He sat by the dying fire with Buster and absentmindedly stroking his head thinking of ways to get revenge. Nothing stupid! Nothing obvious!

Can't take the chance of getting arrested. Bully bastard! Hurting a defenseless woman. I WANT HIS ASS!

He put Buster in the trailer, jumped into the car and drove off. He took the same route that Mabel had taken to the store. He drove back and forth three times at breakneck speed and finally spotted the squad car hoping it was not someone different. He pulled the car between two bushes and watched as Marlowe got out of the squad and walked up to a tree and relieved himself. He stood with his back to Clarence as he wetted the tree. While holding his penis, Clarence snuck up on him and smacked him on his ear.

"What the f...?" He yelled.

"Hi asshole! Let's see what you can do with a man instead of a woman. You piece of shit. He hit him square on the nose and Marlowe reached for his service piece.

"Not man enough to fight me?"

Clarence kicked the gun out of his hand and used an upper cut with his left while the right hand picked up the gun and threw it into the pond. Clarence ripped Marlowe's shirt off and tossed it aside.

"You don't deserve a uniform you piece of shit."

EXTRACTION

Marlowe moaned as he lay on the ground Clarence pulled out his knife and slit Marlowe's clothes in half. As he lay naked, Marlowe curled into a ball. Clarence kicked him in the face and repeatedly in his ribs, making sure that all his injuries matched Mabel's. Marlowe seemed to have passed out from the beating and Clarence searched for his handcuffs. He found them on the belt he had cut in half. The key was in Marlowe's pants pocket. Clarence opened the cuffs and dragged Marlowe to a good sized tree. He propped him on his knees and circled the tree with Marlowe's arms which happened to be the same one he had urinated on before and then he cuffed his hands together. Marlowe looked like he was kissing the tree. Clarence walked back to his car, opened the trunk and took out a can of black spray paint. He sprayed the word S-H-I-T on Marlowe's back. He thought that this was very creative and apropos. He drove the squad car close to the pool, left the engine running and shoved it in. Clarence surveyed his surroundings and was satisfied with his actions.

"Bye, asshole. Explain this to your Lt. and fellow officers. Have a nice day!"

CHAPTER TWENTY-FOUR

Clarence drove back to camp, hooked up the car, checked on Mabel and brought the lawn chairs inside. She was snoring soundly and the bleeding had stopped and ice bag was on the floor. The pills she had gotten for pain would keep her out for while due to her low tolerance.

He carefully pulled out of the campsite and decided to drive straight through to Vegas.

"Where are we?" she asked her voice slurry from the pain-killers.

"Thought we go through Reno and end up in Vegas. I think we need to ditch this camper and the car."

"What did you do?"

"Nothing."

"I'll tell you as soon as we camp for the night. Give me directions if you can."

She rattled the map and traced their route with a finger.

"There's camping in Tahoe or do you want to go to Vegas?"

"Vegas. It's more crowded and we can sell faster."

"OH God! What did you do?" Her voice was a whole pitch higher which meant that she was excited. "We have about thirty miles before a campsite then and I' hungry."

"What do you have a taste for?"

"Ice cream will help with the swelling. O.K. we'll stop-might a well get a for sale sign and stick it in the window."

"Will you tell me over ice cream?"

"Nope, after we camp."

"C'mon."

"Nope."

"Why?"

"You sound like a three year-old."

"C'mooooon."

"NO! Here's a place."

He parked and walked around the car to open her door.

"I'll wait here."

"Okay. Be right back."

He came out with a huge sundae with chocolate dripping sown his hand. The sundae had three scoops of strawberry ice cream and loads of whipping cream.

"Figured nuts would hurt your mouth, so I got extra whipping cream."

She gave him a lopsided grin and dug into the melting mess. Clarence went back into the ice cream parlor and got himself a cone and sat next to her in silence. When he was almost done, a knock came on the window and Clarence saw a little old guy in the most horrible shirt Clarence had never seen. The shirt was green with pink flamingos on it and the short were a sick green.

Clarence opened the door and the man smiled at him and stuck his hand for a shake.

"Eugene Warner, I saw your for sale sign and an inquiring as to what you're asking for the camper. My wife and I retired last month and we want to see the country."

"Car and camper $13,000 firm." Clarence announced.

Eugene asked if he could step inside and Clarence nodded. The little man took a big step and oohed and aahed over the camper.

"I want to bring my wife to see this buy you won't be sitting here, will you?"

"No, we'll be at the campground just outside of town. You're welcome to come there tomorrow if you want."

EXTRACTION

"Any special time?"

"In the morning would be good." Clarence answered. Eugene looked hard at Mabel and Clarence told him that she had some plastic surgery done and would look that way for a while. The man left and waved.

Clarence pulled into the campsite and grabbed the folding chairs and placed them in front of the firepit. He lit some kindling and a few logs caught. Clarence was satisfied and hooked up the electric and water.

"Come out here. I'll start cooking as soon as I tell you."

Mabel moved a little better, he noticed and gingerly sat herself in front of the fire. She stretched her feet toward the flames and asked for a bottle of water. Clarence grabbed one out of the cooler and also gave her an ice bag to place o her face.

"Plastic surgery?" She grinned.

"I wasn't going to explain the whole mess to brother Eugene. It seemed to satisfy him. Good enough. So anyway..."

Mabel couldn't stop the tears. She was laughing and thought her ribs were truly broken now. "Handcuffed to a tree...and broke into another laughing fit.

"The best is for last," he said mysteriously. "I spray painted the word S_HI_I_T on his naked ass and took his clothes and dumped them."

"Oh my God, Clarence. I ca visualize the scene." Still laughing she patted his arm. "How can I ever thank you for the risk you took?"

"I'd do anything for you. I love you woman."

"We do have to sell and quickly before he recuperates. Although he would be stupid to cross the state line. But he is pretty ignorant."

CHAPTER TWENTY-FIVE

Eugene knocked on the door at exactly 8 A.M. and Clarence guessed that he wanted them to move out right now. After much talking and discussion and three cups of coffee later, they had a deal and all would be signed in seven days. This would give them time to find something for them to live in and perhaps haul a beater of a car. Clarence had Mabel lay down and ice her face some more, even though it looked a lot better than it had yesterday. Some of her bruises were starting to turn green and he was fascinated by the colors she could produce on a place background. He smiled at her and got an ice bag for her.

"I'm going to look for a camper. I'll be back in a few hours. Rest."

"He drove into town and checked out a used car lot with no luck. He drove around for a while and spotted a nice Winnebago with a for sale sign on it.

He checked with the owner and found that he wanted nine thousand for it, as is." He looked at the motor and asked the owner to start the engine. He looked for obvious leaks but didn't see anything.

He thanked the man for his patience and drove back to Mabel after picking up some soft Mexican food for her. They discussed the purchase and she said that she still had that much money stashed away and could probably get Eugene to settle faster.

"Let's just do it. We have to get rid of our stuff just to avoid Marlowe and this way poor old Eugene will get stuck with him and he won't be able to find us."

Clarence went back and exchanged money for a title. The man was surprised to see him this soon again. Clarence wheeled and deeled and got the man to settle on $7,500. Clarence drove it to a special car wash and had it washed and waxed. He paid a young kid extra to scrub the inside and three more kids showed up when they saw money exchange hands. Clarence paid out $120.00 to get the cabinets, bathroom and floors scrubbed. One kid was on his hands and knees with a brush scrubbing all the corners of the kitchen area. Clarence gave him an extra twenty. The kid moved on to bedroom cabinets and soon the Winnebago sparkled. Now, he felt that Mabel would not get the

EXTRACTION

urge to start cleaning this thing.

He stopped and bought RV plates and screwed them on. The windows were clean and he felt good about the deal.

She was still sleeping when he came back and parked the thing next to the camper. He grabbed his pole and he and Buster ran down to the water. Within a couple of hours, he had caught four large cat fish and dinner would be on him. He passed some raspberry bushes and thought about desert. He pulled off his t-shirt and filled it with ripe berries, slung it over his shoulder and hiked back.

Mabel smelled the fish cooking and came out of the camper. "I just ate the refried beans and rice and now we have fish. How nice. Who's that?" Her head nodded to the Winnebago.

CHAPTER TWENTY-SIX

The deal was done and all the paperwork was signed on the dotted line. Eugene and his bird-like bride off with the camper and the car.

"I'll miss her." Clarence announced.

"Yeah, I will too."

"We need to work on the Maury thing soon. We have hooked and fish on the hook too long have a way of figuring how to get off of it. I don't want to lose this one because it could get really big."

"Let's send him an the nugget and then call him to see where he stands. They have mines in Wyoming, don't they?"

"Yes, then we'll have a base to work from. Do you want to go now or wait until morning?"

"Let's wait."

They sat close and discussed the plan. What further proof could they show him? What would keep him from doing what they wanted? Would it be

EXTRACTION

better for Mabel to be Mabel and ask for funding for the mine or be anonymous? Which would work to their advantage?

The discussion went on long after all the food was eaten and the wood had burned down to smoldering embers. Mabel was actually starting to doze off when Clarence announced bed time and Buster immediately ran to the nearest tree to relieve himself one more time before going to bed. Mabel stroked him gently behind the ears and agreed it was time for sleep. New sheets were put on the bed and the pillows were soft and fluffy and she was out.

Clarence took his long frame to the hid-a-bed and found that comfort would not be his tonight. He looked around the room and figured what could be done to enhance his sleeping arrangement. If he placed four two-by-fours across the two walls where the couch now sat and did the same thing to the other wall, he could make a bed about six and a half feet long for him. During the day he could throw cushions on it and have a nice long couch. He sat at the table and drew up plans for his project. The two-by-fours would hold up ¾ inch plywood and he could sleep stretched out.

Morning came with a knock on the door. A grizzly looking guy wanted to borrow some water. Clarence pointed to the spigot four feet away from him and told him that was where they got water. The guy nodded and walked to the spigot and turned it on. Water came gushing out. The guy walked to his camper and Mabel saw ten or twelve gallons of water sitting in the window.

"What was that all about?" She wondered.

"He was asking for water and had gallons of it." She was a little afraid of single men driving all over the country, especially after having met the charming serial killer.

"Clarence, why would a guy ask for water if he already has a lot?"

"Maybe it's bath time."

"C'mon."

"I don't know and care less. May be he wants to drown himself."

She slapped him playfully across his head and yelled, "Ouch, that hurts!"

"Sorry, I forgot how delicate you are."

They both laughed.

"Where are you going?" She asked, seeing him check his wallet.

"I want to find a lumber yard and build me a bed. Want to come?"

"No, Buster and I will go to the lake and catch fish

EXTRACTION

you keep losing." She laughed, grabbing her pole, bucket and a chair. "Be careful."

He nodded, waved an drove off.

As she was walking towards the water, the grizzly guy called to her and asked her to hold up. She stopped and Buster made a few noises in his throat while the hair on his back looked like a Mohawk. She was glad to see that Buster conferred with her on this man.

"Yes, what is it?" She coldly asked.

"Do I frighten you?" He asked in return.

"Not at all. Do you want to?"

"That's a strange question." He declared.

"No stranger than yours. What is it you want?"

"I just wanted to talk to you."

"What about?"

"This is going to sound bizarre." He announced.

"Mister, everything you have done and said has been that. Come to the point. I want to fish and not stand here trying to spar with you."

"Let me start over. I'm sorry if I scared you. I was married for thirty years and you look exactly like my late wife. I just wanted to meet you. I'm Richard." He stuck out his hand and she had to wipe hers on her pants before she shook. He reached for his wallet and flipped it open to a picture of Mabel from twenty years ago.

"Oh my. That looks like a twin."

"Yes, I know." He responded. "That's why I had to talk to you. I'm harmless. Where were you raised, if I may ask?"

"Chicago."

"My wife came from California. Have you ever been there?"

"A few weeks ago but that's not what you mean, is it?"

"No. I wondered if you could have been a twin and one was given away."

"You know Richard, I have no clue about that. My mother is dead and so is my father. They were strange people." She found herself softening towards him. "I could have been a triplet for all I know."

"It's strange that I go camping and run across my wife's look-alike."

"Life is strange Richard but I'm not related, I don't think."

"I'm sorry to have bothered you." He walked away with his head hanging down.

She waved and started to put her poles up when she got a beauty of a large mouth bass. He had to be at least twenty two inches. She put him on the stringer and recast in the same spot. "Now one for

Clarence to eat." Within minute, she had another bite. She quickly jerked the rod and had him fighting for freedom. "I'm going to win." The fish fought bravely but she had more experience and finally landed him. He tried to jump out of her hand while she was dislodging the hook but soon had him on the stringer, too. Fishing was too good to quit now so, she again cast in the same spot. Another one was hooked. She totaled all of seven by the time Clarence walked to the lake.

"Do any good," he asked.

"A little." She grinned while yanking on the stringer.

"Good Lord. What did you use for bait?"

"Nightcrawlers, why?"

"They're huge. I never get anything like that."

"I'm better that's all." They both laughed. "But you get to cook them."

"Hey, my mouth is watering already."

CHAPTER TWENTY-SEVEN

She explained what the strange guy had said to her and she wondered if she really was a twin and was never told about it.

"As strange as your mother was, I just wonder if she didn't give one of you away and kept the other one."

"At this point in my life it really doesn't really matter any more. Yes, it would have been fun having a twin sister but I sure would have tried to talk to her out of marrying that man." They both laughed. "We need to overnight Maury that gold nugget and wait for him to take the bait. We can send a picture of a cave and tell him it's in an undisclosed place due to the possibilities. As stupid and greedy as he is, he will be happy not to tell anyone."

They decided to wrap the nugget in a larger box so that Fed Ex would not lose it. They wrapped it in brown paper and shipped it off. "Now we wait." Clarence said, "and then we'll be rich and you can retire from the life of crime. Right Buster?" The dog acted like he understood and wiggled its entire body and barked twice. Mabel swore that he understood every word. The dog dropped down on all fours and refused to move.

"You started it." She replied. "Do you want me to cook?"

"No, I'll get the grill going. I found a new recipe for chicken that I want to try but do we have pineapple?"

"Check the cupboards. I think there is a can left. I'll make the salad."

"What will we do for Christmas?"

"What do you want to do?"

"Make love to you like crazy."

She punched him on the arm and said, "That's not going to happen. Next?"

"I don't understand this."

"Did I ever tell you about Ben?"

"Who's that?"

"Ben and I were buddies. He would call on the spur of the moment and we would go dancing or to dinner. Whatever we did, we had a great time. He never ceased to amuse me and sometimes I would laugh until I cried. We had a blast. He was a huge, well-built man with the most soulful eyes I have ever seen. He was of Mexican and Italian heritage and had the romanticism of both countries. I asked him one day if he was guy. He pulled me off a bar stool and drove to a Hilton hotel. When we got to the room, he started kissing me and fondling my breasts. I was really turned on when he dropped his pants and I realized that I was looking at the world's smallest penis. Even erect, the thing couldn't have measured two inches. I felt a giggle coming on that soon exploded from my mouth into a full-blown roar. He pulled his pants up and left. That was the end of Ben and the end of our friendship. I will not gamble on our relationship."

"Damn, you might as well have cut off his testicles. I guarantee that mine is bigger then two inches."

"I'm sure it is but I don't want to risk what we have and besides, we've been over this numerous times. No more of this or I'll leave you at the side of the road."

"You wouldn't."

"Try me."

"Damn."

"How long do you think it'll be before we hear from our firend?"

EXTRACTION

"No longer than a week, at the most. You know he's greedy."

"I want to get this done and maybe go on vacation."

"We've been on vacation since you sold the house." He laughed.

"I mean a real vacation."

"Like where? Do you have anything in mind?"

"I've always wanted to go to the Bahamas. Sit in the sand and sip an exotic drink with the hotel room to overlook the ocean and fall asleep to the sound of the waves."

"Sounds like heaven. Can I come?"

"Only if you promise not to try anymore funny stuff."

"Cross my heart and hope to die." He crossed his heart and she smiled because she he looked like a little boy making a promise.

"How long before we hear from Maury?" She asked.

"He's so greedy that we'll hear soon. I bet it won't take a week. We need to tell him that we want a cahiers check only."

"Let's get the letter done."

CHAPTER TWENTY-EIGHT

Clarence took the van and disappeared for hours. Mabel wondered what he was up to while having coffee with the neighboring camper. The campers told her the places they had visited and the places they still wanted to see. They were a retired school teacher and her husband was an accountant. Mabel thought they were boring but she was too polite to refuse a good cup of java. The couple was leaving in the morning to go to Arkansas to Crater of Diamonds State Park, to try to find diamonds there. She explained that people from all over the world came there to sift through broken up lava searching for the precious stones. A few weeks ago, a man had found a diamond worth $100,000. Mabel asked many questions and out of the corner of her eye, she saw Clarence pull in the van. She spent another few moment wishing them good luck with the search and told them to be careful driving.

EXTRACTION

The woman hugged Mabel and had tears in her eyes when she said, "It must be hard having a black child."

Mabel had to turn away to keep the woman from seeing her face because she was ready to have a fit of laughter. She waved and walked to her own van.

She opened the door and Clarence yelled, "Do not come in until I say so."

"What are you doing?"

"Go away!" He yelled.

"Come on Buster, we'll go for a walk. She headed towards the woods and Buster spotted a rabbit which, of course, he chased. She wondered if he'd eat it if it was caught. She shook her head and believed her dog was much more civilized than that. Can dogs be civilized? She smiled to herself. Now, the dog went after a squirrel who was smart enough to head up the tree and Mabel broke out in laughter at the two creature's antics. She called Buster and started towards the van.

Clarence stood on the steps with his arms crossed looking very patient.

She yelled, "Can we come in now?"

Clarence grinned from ear to ear and nodded. She opened the door and was hit with the smell of pine.

The cutest little Christmas tree was standing on the end table, completely decorated. Under the tree, were wrapped gifts.

"Oh my," she said. "This is amazing. How did you do all this?" She was awed.

"Well, you seemed to have forgotten that tomorrow is Christmas and I wanted to surprise you."

"I certainly am surprised by all this. You're right. I totally forgot. I was so caught up with the whole Maury thing that it completely slipped my mind. You're wonderful." She kissed him on the cheek.

"I could be more wonderful if you let me."

"No! You're wonderful just as you are. Now, I'd like to go to the store for a nice roast. Want to come?"

"You're making my favorite dinner? WOW! I think I'll be nice from now on."

"Let's go."

She went to the store and he stayed with Buster in the van. She shortly came out with two huge bags of groceries. He jumped up to help her and she said that she was fine and sat in the passenger seat.

"You will have a meal to die for tomorrow." She promised.

"I can't wait. I love pot roast."

"You love food."

"Never denied that." He grinned.

"Did you celebrate it on Christmas Eve or Christmas day?"

She asked him, "We opened presents on Christmas day but had a super meal on Christmas Eve. How about you?"

"It was sporadic at our house. After my brother died, no one wanted to celebrate the Holidays. I was all but forgotten. Sometimes I got gifts but mostly I got nothing but a drunken mother." She laughed but the pain came through.

"I'm sorry for that little girl."

"Yes, I am too. With Buddy, we had Christmas all day. We played with his toys and the year he got his first bike, I ran up and down the block with him. We never forgot that we only had each other until he got married. Then, I was forgotten again. I sometimes wonder if it is me."

"No, it's not you. It's them. You are a warm, wonderful person."

"Stop being mushy." She laughed.

"Seriously. You are."

"Can I open my presents?"

"Tomorrow."

"Why."

"Because tomorrow is Christmas. You have to go to bed before Santa comes."

"Oh, for crying out loud."

"Go to bed. Tomorrow will be here soon enough."

CHAPTER TWENTY-NINE

Like a young child, she jumped out of bed eager to open her presents. She smelled coffee brewing and was greeted with a big smile and a big cup.

"Merry Christmas, sunshine." He grinned at her. "I know you need coffee before anything else."

"Sorry, bad habit, I guess." She sipped the warm brew and eagerly eyed the presents still under the tree. She sat on the couch and finished her first cup in silence.

He handed her a neatly wrapped package and said, "From me to you."

She tore the wrapping off and oohed and aahed at the shiny earrings in the small velvet box.

"Silver. You really know what I like."

He handed her another one that looked like a clothing box. She unwrapped it and found a t-shirt that said, "Here fishy, fishy" on the front of it. She laughed and asked him if he was jealous of her getting bigger fish than him. He just laughed at her.

He handed her one more and said, "That's the last one." She saw a map-like instrument and had no idea what it was. Her puzzled expression made him laugh as he explained that it was a navigator. That she could put any address in it and it would tell her how to get there. She absolutely loved it once he explained and showed her everything.

She went to the bedroom and came out with a few gifts of her own. She handed him the first one and he said, "No way! You didn't forget about Christmas. You con artist."

He ripped the paper off the small box and found a Rolex watch.

"Oh my Lord! I have never had anything this beautiful in my life." He stated.

"You deserve good things. You're a good man." She smiled.

"You spent too much on me but I love it." He was like a little kid with a new toy. Did you know that I can set the time for three continents on this? Wow. This is the greatest present I ever got. Thanks, Mabel."

"You're very welcome. Here's your last one." She handed him a box ornately wrapped in gold.

He ripped it open and saw the t-shirt which said,

"The worst day of fishing beats the best day at work.

They both laughed until tears streamed down their cheeks.

"You got me one and I got you one." They started laughing all over again.

"I think we should wear them every Christmas from now on." Clarence stated, 'We can start our own tradition."

"Great idea. I'll go put mine on." She took it into the bedroom and came back out wearing it proudly. He had his on and they could not stop laughing.

"Well, even though it doesn't feel like Christmas, I should start the roast and we can have dinner around two. How does that sound?"

"Fine, you know me, I'll eat whenever the food is put out. What can I do to help?"

"Take the dog out and then give him his gift." He then noticed one final gift under the tree. He called Buster and they went for a walk.

By the time he came back, the oven was on and she was making gravy. She handed Buster his gift and he tore the wrapping off to discover a huge raw hide bone. He placed it in his mouth and tried to go through the doorway into the bedroom. They both started laughing when the dog looked confused that it wouldn't fit. Buster turned sideways but the bone stayed straight and he still could not go through the door. He dropped the bone and pulled it into the bedroom.

"Damn that dog is smart." She said. He nodded in agreement.

"It's almost like he knew that it wouldn't go through without him pulling it through."

"That dog is uncanny sometimes. I guess he'll get Christmas dinner too."

"He deserves it. He is good dog and never messes the house or chews things like other

dogs. I often wonder where he came from."

"He deserves it. He is a good dog and never messes the house or chews things like other dogs. I often wonder where he came from."

"I don't think we know the half of what he is capable of."

"O.K. You can peel potatoes and I'll do the carrots."

They worked in silence until he turned on the radio and the camper was flooded with carols. They sang along comfortably, all the while peeling rooted veggies.

The meal went without incident and they decided to take a walk through the woods for Buster to let out some energy. Clarence, full of good food ran ahead and allowed Buster to catch up. Then he would chase Buster and the dog actually hid behind a tree but Clarence found him and laughed. The dog ran, Clarence ran and Mabel shayedshayed along at a gentle pace letting neither dog, nor man upset her full stomach. She wondered what the mail would bring tomorrow and if they could actually go to the Bahamas and sit in the sun. The temp here was about a comfortable sixty but she liked her dusting snow on Christmas. She kind of missed the change of the seasons back in Illinois but did not miss driving on ice and the sliding into trees. She did love spring and the promise of things to yet, come. She loved the flowers and the smell of newly cut grass but the adventure with Clarence was fun and exciting.

Buster took a time out to do his duty and was obviously ready to go home. Clarence started a fire in the pit and they roasted marshmallows and she laughed. She realized that she was content with this man and dog. She wanted for nothing and had no urges to do anything stupid for a while. She thought about the risks she had taken when desperation was in her every waking moment. She realized that she did not want to die anymore but wanted to experience new things and new places.

"Deep thoughts?" He asked looking at her head, while she was staring into the sky.

"Just thinking about how comfortable I am with you and Buster."

'Well, let's get married."

"Not that comfortable," she laughed.

"You don't know what you're missing."

"I'm ready for bed. Too much Christmas, too much wine, too much food. I'm tired."

She walked to his chair and kissed his forehead.

"Merry Christmas, good night."

"Merry Christmas to you, too. I could warm your bed."

"Night dear."

She left him sitting alone by the fire. Very few people camped at Christmas and she wondered where everyone went at this time of year. There must be fifteen hundred camp sites here and at the most, forty campers. The same place in the summer would be filled to the max. She brushed her teeth and went to bed.

CHAPTER THIRTY

Mabel woke to the smell of frying bacon and the odor of coffee reached her brain at the same time. She stretched and decided that she was starving for bacon and needed her coffee like an empty gas tank needs gas. She ran through the shower and put on her fishing t-shirt and a pair of jeans. Clarence seemed to have the breakfast under control and handed her a cup of coffee just the way she liked it.

"Morning Ma'am. What'll you have for eats?" He grinned at her.

"Let me have my two cups first. Bye the way yesterday was one of the best Christmas' I ever had."

"My pleasure." He knew not to converse with her before she had her second cup. He sat and inhaled the food like a starving war orphan. He ate three scrambled eggs, four pieces of toast and numerous strips of bacon. He burped quietly and decided another couple of pieces of toast would hit the spot. He waited by the toaster for it to give up his food and lavishly buttered it and wolfed it down.

Mabel finished her second cup and asked him if he had seen the mailman. He shook his head but said, "I was not watching for him but I'll take a walk and see what's in the box."

She grunted a reply and decided a third cup would do her a world of good. Clarence whistled for the dog and they trotted up the road.

He and the dog were back in a short time and he howled like a wolf.

"Merry Christmas, again" as he thrust the letter from Maury at her. She ripped it open and her mouth dropped. A cashier's check for 495,000 thousand dollars was enclosed with a short note asking her to let him know as soon as the gold was removed from the mine.

"He kept five thousand." She grumbled.

"Damn woman, we got a half a million what more do you want?"

"Tickets to the Bahamas."

"O.K. Let's go get them.

"I want to eat first."

He scrambled her eggs and put the toast in just before the eggs were done. He buttered it for her and spread grape jelly all over it. She had taught him that jelly needed to reach all corners of the toast. He smiled while he did his chores for her. He started cleaning the frying pan while she ate calmly and watched him. The check was in her pants pocket and they would go to town and cash it later. They would get tickets and fly to the Bahamas and drink pink drinks and bask in the sun.

Clarence went into the bedroom closet to get a light jacket when she felt a rumbling beneath her feet. She looked out the front window and saw nothing, but the door burst open and there he stood with a baseball bat in one hand and a knife in the other. He glared at her and hit her in the mouth with the small end of the bat. She felt herself go light headed as she was spitting out teeth.

"Damn Marlowe," she thought, "we are never going to be rid of him."

"Bitch, I lost my wife, kids, and job because of you. I'm going to hurt you real bad."

She wondered where Clarence was and why he didn't respond to the noise and Marlowe's yelling. He pulled a roll of duct tape from his jacket and tied her hands and feet with it. He struck her a few more times in the face and kicked her in her ribs. Even though she fought them, the tears trickled down her face. The pain was excruciating and the blood mingled with tears. She was hog tied and helpless. No Clarence to the rescue. Where was he?

Marlowe stacked books and newspapers in the middle of the room and smashed whatever was in his way. He was out of control and very dangerous. Now, he had no police department to keep him in check. Would he kill her? She no longer wanted to die. She wanted to go to the Bahamas. She struggled futilely against the duct tape until her shoulders wanted to scream with pain. She watched him kick in their pathetic television and stomp on the AM/FM radio until small pieces of plastic were the only hint that this had once been a radio.

Still no Clarence. Why was she alone? Where did he go? Did he sneak out the door and go for help? God, her head hurt. It felt as though she was hit by a train. Her body ached. She was rolling on the floor trying to get to the door when he kicked her again and she felt something pop in her inside. Where was the dog?

Marlowe cut up cushions and placed the stuffing on the paper pile.

"OH, God! He is going to burn me alive." She thought miserably. Marlowe tore up books, newspapers and pulled the curtains from the windows all in frenzy as someone who had the devil after him. He kept looking around frantically for other things to pile onto the pyre he was going to have.

Mabel heard some type of thumping from the bedroom and wondered if Clarence was in the same situation as she. She tried to make some sounds but the duct tape was too tight over her mouth and did not allow for loud noises. Her pain in the side was getting worse and her head felt like it might come off her shoulders. She wondered if she had a broken rib that might have punctured her lung. No, her breathing seemed to be OK except that it was shallow due to the tape. She heard a crashing noise and then passed out.

She woke up to find Clarence sitting on the floor next to her cradling her head in his lap. Tears were running down his face as he stroked her cheek. Buster sat in front of him with the cell phone in his mouth. Marlowe was on his stomach with handcuffs on him and four bulky state troopers surrounded him as Mabel passed out.

She woke up in a sterile setting and she knew, by the smell, that she was in the hospital. She felt her forehead and felt only gauze. Her ribs were taped and there was a dull, throbbing pain in her head. "Oh God," she thought. "I almost died. That creep was going to burn her to death and no one was around.

She heard a soft tapping on the door and Clarence's face appeared. He looked tired and worn out. Just like she felt.

"Thank you." She murmured.

"It was Buster who came and got me." He replied softly as though a loud voice would further injure her.

"I love both of you guys."

"So, OK, then. Let's get married."

"No, I like us just fine the way we are. I want to go to the Bahamas."

"Could you leave Buster in a kennel? After what he did?"

"No."

"We'll go to Florida and that way he can be with us."

"That will do fine. When do I get out of here? Have you spoken to the doctor?"

"Yeah, he said that Sandy will be fine. That she has mostly bruises and the broken ribs. A good bump on the head and three loose teeth."

"You know that I don't have insurance and Sandy

is as good name as any other."

"You will be released, probably, tomorrow. Then we can make our way to Florida but we have t come back for the trial."

"We'll come back because I want to see him go down for life."

She tried to smile but her mouth was sore and she gave what appeared to be a grimace. He patted her hand and told her he loved her. She nodded but felt like her head was going to come off her shoulders.

"I need a vacation. Somewhere warm and calm. And most of all, I want to get out of here."

"Same old Mabel. Oops, I mean Sandy."

They laughed and planned their next trip.